JILL RUBALCABA

# THE WADJET EYE

CLARION BOOKS
NEW YORK

Clarion Books
a Houghton Mifflin Company imprint
215 Park Avenue South, New York, NY 10003
Copyright © 2000 by Jill Rubalcaba
First Clarion paperback edition, 2006.

The text was set in 11-point Nofret.

www.houghtonmifflinbooks.com

Printed in the U.S.A.

*Library of Congress Cataloging-in-Publication Data*

Rubalcaba, Jill.
The wadjet eye / by Jill Rubalcaba.
p.    cm.
Includes bibliographical reference ( ).
Summary: After his mother dies, Damon, a young medical
student living in Alexandria, Egypt, in 45 B.C., makes perilous
journey to Spain to locate his father, who is serving in the
Roman army led by Julius Caesar.
ISBN: 0-395-68942-2
1. Egypt—History—332–30 B.C.—Juvenile fiction. 2. Rome—History—
Republic, 265–30 B.C.—Juvenile fiction. [1. Egypt—History—
332–30 B.C.—Fiction. 2. Rome—History—Republic, 265–30 B.C.—Fiction.
3. Voyages and travels—Fiction. 4. Adventure and adventures—Fiction.]
I. Title.
PZ7.R8276  Wad  2000    [Fic]—dc21
99057744

CL ISBN-13: 978-0-395-68942-4   CL ISBN-10: 0-395-68942-2
PA ISBN-13: 978-0-618-68927-9   PA ISBN-10: 0-618-68927-3

DOM  10 9 8 7 6 5 4 3

For Dan—
it's my good fortune to have you by my side.
And for Kelly and Danny,
who make the journey so much fun.

# EGYPT
## 45 B.C.

# ONE

Even before Damon came fully awake, he knew she was dead. Her hand felt cold and stiff in his. He didn't open his eyes, just waited for the tears. But they didn't come.

Instead, frustration welled into the back of his throat until he thought he would choke. What good were his studies if he couldn't cure his own mother? The root he'd brought home from medical school and mashed with mortar and pestle had done nothing for her pain. He hadn't even been able to spare her that.

The Pharaoh's own physician, Damon's teacher, Olympus, lectured long on the miracles of modern medicine. Where were the miracles for his mother? Damon hadn't found them. His notes on Praxagoras's theories on blood vessels lay rolled in the corner. Had they saved her? No. She had died anyhow.

Damon had known from the beginning he couldn't stop the thing that grew inside her. He had seen many die this way. The one lump had borne more, extending her stomach outward as if she were pregnant. But no child grew there. All the theories in the Museum combined could not even give her comfort in the end. Why did he study if it all came to this?

Her hand felt as if it were sucking the heat from his own, as if death were spreading up his arm. Gently, he twisted his hand, trying to free it from her fingers that had frozen clutching his. He stopped. Images came to him of his fellow students breaking the fingers off corpses in search of riches hidden by their death grasp. Would her fingers snap? He couldn't leave his hand in hers forever. He pulled again—carefully.

His hand slipped from hers. Her fingers circled nothing now. He covered her open hand with his own and smoothed it. When the stiffness passed, he would place her hands on her heart. Now he could do nothing. All along he had been able to do nothing. Damon covered his face with his hands, massaging his temples with his fingertips. He'd done nothing but watch her waste away.

In the swirl of thoughts that spun and wouldn't rest, a noise surfaced. Knocking. It must have been continuing for some time. He had heard, but he had not heard.

Damon stood stiffly, kneading his lower back with his thumbs. It ached from his having slept so long in the chair. He left his mother's sleeping chamber, closing the door behind him. Who would call so late? He was startled when he saw light streaming through the arches of the inner walls. Was it morning? The knock turned to pounding. Damon thrust open the door, annoyed at the intrusion.

His friend Artemas filled the doorway. "I checked the Museum first. They said you hadn't been there for days. I was worried."

Damon had stood up too fast. He leaned against the wall, waiting for the shadows that clouded his vision to pass. He could see the tall outline of Artemas's muscular frame and the white of his tunic, but the familiar face was blurred. Damon could only make out the curl of his wavy hair and the bend of his hawk nose.

"Are you all right?" Artemas asked.

"She has crossed to the other bank."

"I'm sorry."

Damon nodded. He didn't trust his voice. Especially with Artemas. Artemas was like a brother. Damon couldn't remember a time when he hadn't known him. Their mothers told the story of how they had crawled for each other in the market seventeen years ago. As if even as babies they knew that their fates were connected.

Now their mothers must be telling that same story in the Field of Reeds, where Artemas and he could not hear them.

When he saw the tears fill Artemas's eyes, Damon looked away. Why couldn't *he* cry? Artemas was the physically strong one—nearly twice Damon's size. Damon was as thin and weak as a papyrus reed, and yet Artemas could weep— why couldn't he?

Damon reached under the stone bench for his sandals. "I must summon the embalmers. She wanted to be prepared in the way of the ancients."

"I can go get them for you, or if you would rather, I could stay." Artemas looked past Damon to the closed door of the death chamber. He swallowed. "Or I could go . . ."

Why in the name of Ra did Artemas want to become a soldier if he was so afraid of blood and death? The young assistants in the dissection rooms at the Museum weren't as squeamish, and they were no more than ten years old.

"I'll stay with her," Damon said. He walked Artemas to the courtyard and watched him pass through the gate and disappear in the twists of the lane that led to the center of town.

Damon turned to go back inside the villa. For the span of one heartbeat he expected to hear his mother's cheerful greeting. He felt his heart stop when no greeting came, and then pain filled his chest when his heart began to beat again.

Damon went back to the gate. He tucked his straight black hair behind his ears and leaned his head between the iron rods, feeling the coolness on his temples. He closed his eyes and waited for Artemas to return with the embalmers.

# TWO

W e cannot prepare her." The embalmer quickly backed toward the gate in the courtyard.

Damon followed the embalmer, clutching at his linen tunic. "But why? I have plenty of gold, if that's your worry. We've saved for this." He could give him the Venetian glass, too. There was plenty to pay the man.

"It's not a question of gold. You'll find no one who will touch her." The embalmer extended his palms to Damon helplessly. "The plague . . ."

"But she did not die from a plague."

Artemas stepped behind the embalmer, blocking his exit. He stood with arms crossed over his broad chest. "There has been no plague in this house."

"The sores . . ." The embalmer looked from Artemas to Damon.

"Those are just bedsores," Damon pleaded. "She was sick for a very long time. Toward the end she could barely move. Besides, you know there has been no outbreak of plague in Alexandria for months."

"We cannot be sure," whined the embalmer.

"But I can. I've been with her. She had no plague."

"We cannot risk it. We cannot bring her to the Beautiful House. Her body should be burned, the way of the barbarians."

Damon flinched. His father was Roman; that made Damon half, as the embalmer said, barbarian.

"But she was Egyptian."

The embalmer shrugged. "You could take her to the desert. Before coffins, it was done that way. The sands will preserve her."

"And risk the jackals digging her up and tearing her apart? Her ka condemned to roam the Red Land forever?" Damon wanted to strike the man.

"Cover her with stones. They may not dig her up."

"Get out." Damon held up his hand to stop the man's babble. He'd hear no more.

"I am not to blame." The embalmer backed into Artemas. Artemas stepped aside, and the embalmer fell on his backside. He scrambled on his hands and knees out into the street.

The months of frustration boiled up in Damon. Months of failure. He slammed the gate behind the embalmer. He pulled it open and slammed it again. The pin crumbled the mortar in the wall, and still he slammed it. He slammed it until the top pin came free and the gate hung from the bottom pin at a dangerous angle. Artemas grabbed Damon around the waist with one arm, hoisting him off his feet.

Damon struggled against Artemas, kicking the air. He might as well have struggled against Ra. "Let me go!"

But Artemas held tight. Finally, Damon went limp, and Artemas lowered him to the ground. Damon cursed the gods, cursed Anubis and his embalmers, cursed himself. He had failed his mother again.

# THREE

"You can do it." Artemas paced the courtyard.

"Embalm her?" Damon shook his head. "I can't."

"Why not? You're a physician, aren't you?"

"My own mother?" Damon sat down hard on the stone bench. He pushed the hair out of his eyes and rubbed the back of his neck.

Artemas bent down, his face close to Damon's. "Do you have a better idea?"

"I've never even seen an embalming."

"There's the desert, then. Enough rocks . . ."

Damon clenched his fists. "The scavengers are sure to rip her body to shreds. Without her body, her ka will have no place to go . . . for eternity."

"Then the Roman way. You're half Roman."

"I may be tainted with Roman blood, but *she* wasn't. She never understood the Roman ways."

Damon shook his head. "And I never understood why she loved him. They were so different."

"You're different from your father, but surely *you* love him?"

"I don't know him."

"But—"

"You wouldn't understand. Your father sits with you for the evening meal each night. I can't even remember what my father looks like."

"A soldier's life is full of sacrifice."

"What of *our* sacrifice?" Damon bit back his anger and spoke with forced control. "My mother died without him. Alone."

"But she wasn't alone. She had you with her. And now you are not alone. I'm here. And I can help you prepare her for her journey to the otherworld. Just tell me what to do."

Damon slammed his open palms onto the edge of the stone seat, skinning the heels of his hands. "We have to cut her open, from her neck to her navel. Then hollow her out like a gourd. Do you think you can help me do that? Do you?"

Artemas went pale. Damon felt sorry that he had pushed Artemas, exposing his weakness. Artemas was only trying to help. Damon was angry at his father, not at Artemas. Why wasn't his father here? Why did Damon always have to be responsible? Just once, he wished he could let someone else take charge.

Artemas sat beside him and spoke evenly, as if he were trying to reason with a young child. "What was your mother is gone. Her ba has left. What remains is only flesh and bone. You must prepare the body for her ka's return in the after-world. That was her belief. Don't think beyond that."

Damon rubbed his temples. "You're right. I'm sorry. I should be thinking of her." Damon squeezed Artemas's shoulder. "You're a good friend." Damon noticed that Artemas's face was still as colorless as the desert midday. "Put your head between your knees until the dizziness passes."

Artemas sat with his head low.

Now Damon paced. Artemas was right. He *could* do it. Herodotus had written in detail about embalming. It wasn't that difficult. The materials would be easy to get. It could be done. Damon felt his energy surging. He could help her now.

Artemas lifted his head. "You're going to do it, aren't you?"

Damon nodded.

"How will you know what to do?"

"Herodotus has written about the process." Behind Artemas the gate hung awkwardly. What had he done? This wasn't like him. Artemas was the one who smashed things. Damon shook his head. "Here, give me a hand."

"I know of Herodotus. He was a Greek. But what does a historian know about cutting up a body?" Artemas leaned into the heavy iron gate with his shoulder, preparing to lift it back into place.

"Maybe not the cutting so much, but how to prepare the organs and the flesh." Damon saw Artemas pale again. "Now, don't faint on me. This gate would probably crush both of us." Damon helped Artemas raise the heavy gate. The hinge pin wavered over the opening in the wall.

Artemas steadied the gate. "Herodotus wrote more than four hundred years ago. There have to be more modern methods." The pin dropped to the left of the hole. They lifted the gate again.

"A moment ago you were the one trying to talk me into this." Damon grunted. His arms ached.

"I just thought there would be some new way . . ."

"Mummification hasn't changed—umph, hold it still, will you?—all that much in thousands of years." The pin dropped into place. Damon shook his arms by his sides. The ache receded. "We'll need cedar oil, beeswax, juniper berries, and natron—lots of natron. The rest I'll have to look up." Damon brushed away bits of sand and crumbled mortar from his shoulder. "Oh, and palm wine to wash the intestines." Artemas paled again. He sat and put his head back between his legs.

Damon left the courtyard, clapping the dust from his hands. He returned cradling four vases. "When she knew her time was near, she chose the coffins for the liver, lungs, stomach, and intestines. The inscriptions are beautiful."

Damon knew that Artemas did not understand the hieroglyphs carved into the alabaster, but the head of Anubis, protector of the dead, would be familiar.

"How can you tell one from the other?" Artemas asked.

"One what?"

Artemas swallowed hard. "Organ."

"I've taken anatomy at the Museum. Since Herophilis, there have been many studies. It is quite clear, actually." Damon placed the vases on the bench.

"Then the things I have heard of those studies are true?"

Damon knew what Artemas meant. He too had heard the rumors—murmurings about instructors and zealous students cutting open living humans to see the heart pump, the lungs inflate, the nerves twitch. He had seen the lamps glow in the middle of the night and wondered, but he had no proof. He shrugged.

Artemas curled his lip. "Battle, at least, has honor."

Damon did not feel like arguing about this

again. Artemas would always have the same ridiculous, idealized notion about honor accompanying death in battle. When Artemas held a dying man in his arms, he'd feel differently, Damon was sure.

Artemas lifted the lid of a vase and peered inside. "So, *can* you do it?"

Damon nodded. He wanted to say "Of course," but his voice failed him. His friend would know he was bluffing, anyhow. They'd find out soon enough if he could do it.

# FOUR

**D**amon leaned over the corpse of his mother with the scalpel poised, the point inches above the navel. A linen shroud covered her face and all but the place he planned to incise.

He'd done dozens of examinations after death. He closed his eyes and visualized himself in anatomy class. *This is just a lesson,* he repeated. *Just another cadaver, like all the others.* He opened his eyes but still could not cut.

Her skin looked powdery, as if ash had fallen from the sky and coated her body. This was the woman who had chased him with a broom when he had broken an amphora while practicing juggling—not some nameless body. The woman who had fought the director of the Museum to get him admitted when everyone else felt it should be honor enough for him to be a scribe.

He lifted the shroud at her shoulder. The

scarab tattoo seemed to stand away from her skin, the ink dark against the paleness. The scarab appeared to struggle to free itself from her dead body. Damon remembered her as she was before the sickness, kneading bread dough on the marble slab in the kitchen, the scarab moving over the motion of her muscles. Moving in time to the songs she sang while she worked. When he was little, he used to pretend it was a live beetle she kept as a pet on her shoulder.

Damon lowered the linen. He closed his eyes again. He could not think of this body as some nameless corpse, but it was no longer his mother, either. The mother he had known was with Anubis. This was just a shell, left here for safe-keeping until her ka could return. He must prepare it for her life in the afterworld.

He stood back, his weight on his heels, and breathed deep the smell of roses. He had scattered petals from her favorite roses over the floor, and as he prepared the work area around the table, his feet had crushed the delicate petals, releasing their scent. The four vases that would hold the cleansed organs stood on the floor. Damon had filled each one with dried herbs and placed them by the basins of palm wine. All was ready. It was time.

He whispered, "Thoth, give me the strength,"

and pressed the blade into the flesh. A thin red line followed his blade. The cut was made.

"Are you all right in there?" Artemas yelled through the door.

Damon spread the incision open and worked quickly now. He held his breath against the foul odor and tried to remember the rose petals' smell. Cupping both hands, he scooped the intestines and sloshed them over the side into a shallow dish of palm wine. He cut them free and set the dish aside.

"Damon?"

"I don't think we have enough natron," Damon called back. He took shallow breaths through his mouth, but even so, the stench of death, death from a long sickness, overpowered him. Artemas would topple like a column at the temple of Karnak if he came into the room now.

When they had prepared the sleeping chamber, Artemas had kept up a constant babble. They'd brought a table from the medical school and jars for draining the bodily fluids and scalpels for removing the organs. Artemas had talked rapidly about nothing while Damon sharpened the blades—anything to keep his mind off the task at hand. It had wearied Damon. He'd wanted quiet.

There was enough natron to dry two corpses, but Damon needed to keep Artemas busy until he removed the brain through the nostrils with the picks he had hidden from Artemas in the folds of his kilt. Artemas would have gone down for sure if he had known the purpose of those tools.

"Another sack, I think, and some powder of myrrh as well," Damon shouted at the closed door. His eyes stung and watered, and he fought the urge to gag.

"I'll be back shortly."

*Not too shortly*, Damon thought. Powder of myrrh would be hard to come by this time of year. Ships were not traveling yet, though winter was nearly over.

"Damon?"

"Yes?" Damon struggled to keep the annoyance out of his voice.

"Are you all right?"

Would Artemas just leave? Damon didn't want to think about whether he was all right or not. "Just go. I'm going to be fine." He had no choice. He didn't want to be fine. But he had no choice.

# FIVE

W e didn't need the natron after all," Damon
    said.

Artemas swung the amphora from his shoulder
and positioned it near Damon, who sat on the
bench overlooking the garden.

"She's surrounded with it," Damon said. "Now
we must wait—the drying will take time."

"Was it difficult?"

What did Artemas think? Of course it was difficult. He shrugged.

The two sat staring into the garden. The bust
of Caesar, a gift from Damon's father, seemed to
look down on them from the pedestal rising out
of the roses.

Damon felt irritable; even the statues annoyed
him. "This courtyard looks just like Alexandria—
less and less Egyptian."

"Since when has Alexandria been anything
like the rest of Egypt?"

Damon grunted. How could he argue? Alexandria and Rome had more in common than Alexandria and the rest of her country. He, like most Alexandrians, had never felt the heat of the desert, nor seen the Nile overflow its banks during the inundation. But he felt like arguing. "Alexandria attracts nothing but pirates."

Artemas fingered Damon's silk tunic. "It seems their trade goods aren't beneath you."

"It wasn't the debtors and criminals who wove this fabric. They're all in your blessed army." Damon knew it rankled Artemas that Alexandria took in any outlaw at its gate who would enlist. Maybe now Artemas would fight with him. He felt like shouting at someone.

"It's a challenge to lead men unaccustomed to following orders. Cleopatra's officers must be true leaders."

"What is it with you today?" Damon threw up his hands. "Have you no fight in you?"

"I know what you're trying to do." Artemas sniffed. "It's not me that angers you. Why don't we talk about what really bothers you?"

"I miss the old days." Damon wanted to say, *when my mother lived.* But it was more than that. He missed boyhood, when his cares were few. "I miss the old market."

"When it was safe for crawling babies to

explore and, if the gods smiled, maybe even find a friend?"

Damon felt his anger dissolve. He could never stay angry with Artemas. With his bare foot he covered the design of the spider woven into the thick Persian carpet his father had sent from Zela. The battle there had been so swift and crushing that Caesar had announced to the world, *"Veni, vidi, vici."* Everyone knew what those words meant. Even Damon, who knew no Latin, could translate them: *I came, I saw, I conquered.* Damon had felt proud that his father had been there with Caesar, but he would not admit it to anyone. Not even to Artemas, who had carved the words into a crocodile hide and stretched it across a frame to hang over his sleeping pallet.

Damon smoothed the fringed edge of the carpet. The pride had dwindled over time, like everything else—the anticipation of his father's return, even the love for his father. He felt nothing.

Pivoting on his heel, he brushed the carpet with the ball of his foot. The silk threads glittered in the sun. "I must send word to my father."

"You're going to tell him in a letter that your mother died?"

Damon shrugged. Why did Artemas make it sound so terrible? "What else can I do?"

"You can go to him. Tell him face to face."

"What for?"

"Because he's your father, and he deserves to hear it from you."

"He doesn't care about me."

"You don't know that."

"Do you see my father anywhere? If he cared, he'd be here. With us."

"I see your father everywhere." Artemas looked around the courtyard at the gifts Damon's father had sent.

"These . . . *things*," Damon said with disgust, "don't make up for his not being here. For his never being here."

"Your mother loved him."

"She was going to meet him in Italy after the sowing. He retires this year. He was to claim his legionnaire's pension, a farm."

"Then you'll go instead."

"I have my studies."

"When you get back, you can continue. It would be good for you to see him. Where is he now?"

"With Caesar, always with his Caesar." Damon picked a small stone from beneath the bench and pegged it at the bust.

Artemas grabbed his arm. "Would you show disrespect to your men of medicine? Would you toss a stone at Hippocrates? Don't dishonor a man I admire."

"I'm sorry," Damon said. "It's just . . ." He closed his eyes. "I've never even been out of Alexandria."

"It took great courage to do what you did for your mother. This trip will be nothing in comparison."

"It's a different kind of courage." *Your kind,* thought Damon.

"I'll go with you. Together we'll find your father."

"What about Cleopatra's navy? I thought you were going to enlist."

"The timbers are still not here from Byblos. It will be two years before her navy is seaworthy."

"You would go all the way across the sea with me?" Why was he surprised? Artemas would go anywhere for no reason at all.

"It will be an adventure, wait and see," Artemas said.

"That's what I am afraid of."

# SIX

Artemas strode along the docks, hopping over thick hemp lines and dodging merchants who shouldered rolled-up carpets. Damon picked his way behind, tripping on nets and bumping into tall red clay amphoras that lined the boardwalks. The first ships of the season, anchored in the harbor, lay low at their water lines with full cargo holds.

Men bartered in Greek. Damon heard very few speaking Egyptian, fewer still Latin. He would have to learn some Latin on the voyage—enough to travel the countryside at least. Enough to greet his father.

Artemas pointed to a ship anchored near the lighthouse. "The sailors say she's headed toward Spain."

"Spain?"

"Caesar's forces are gathered there. That's where your father must be."

"But *Spain?*" Damon was sure that must be near the edge of civilization. Caesar would not go so far west. What could possibly be gained?

"She's a Roman galley, for sure," Artemas went on. "Look how awkward her bow is."

It looked like all the other ships to Damon, except a bit shabbier.

Artemas shook his head. "Probably suffering rot-worm, too."

Why was Artemas sounding so cheerful? "If the boat is so horrible, why are we considering it?" Damon didn't like the sound of rot-worm. He pointed to a cluster of solid-looking vessels pulling on their anchor lines. "What about one of those?"

Artemas smiled. "You have a good eye. Those are Greek. Now *we* know how to build a ship. How to sail, too. Not like the Romans. No offense intended."

"None taken. I'm sure I have no sea legs—I'll blame that on my Roman half." *Along with all my other faults,* Damon thought. "Must we take that one?"

"I'm afraid the Roman dog is the only one going our way."

Artemas called to a boy unloading a dinghy. "You, are you from that Roman vessel?"

The boy looked to where Artemas pointed, and nodded.

"Is your captain on board?"

The boy looked puzzled for a moment, then he pointed. Artemas and Damon followed his outstretched finger to a group of men bent over charts spread open across a block of granite. They walked over to the men, who were sharing news of the trade winds.

"Be careful," one man was saying. "The shoal has shifted here. We saw the skeleton of a ship run aground. It will have broken up by now, and there'll be no marker for you."

The other captains marked their charts—all except one, who was biting off chunks of lamb from a bone he grasped in his right hand. His left held a cup of wine.

The man across from Artemas looked up at him. Despite his height, Artemas stood on tiptoe, craning his neck at their charts.

"Move along. There's nothing for you to see here," one of the men ordered gruffly.

Damon turned to go, but Artemas grabbed him by the elbow. "My friend and I are waiting to speak with the captain of the Roman ship."

The man with the lamb bone pointed it at him. Grease shone from his chin. "And what if he does not want to speak with you?"

"Then he'll be missing an opportunity to take a ship's physician aboard." Artemas gestured toward Damon. Damon straightened up the best he could, although he didn't know why. What did he care how these scruffy seamen saw him?

Artemas went on like a merchant selling from his booth, only it was Damon he was trying to market. "He studies under Cleopatra's own physician. I hear that your oarsmen are suffering from disease."

Damon looked at Artemas. Where had he heard that? Probably playing a hunch—oarsmen were always suffering from something. The confines of the hold and the demands of the rowing bred illness.

Artemas stepped in front of Damon. "And I can organize your men for battle in case of a pirate attack."

The captains laughed. "You are a bit young to have much experience in warfare, aren't you?" said the man who had spoken first.

Artemas bristled. "Old enough."

*Not old enough,* Damon thought. He knew Artemas was sensitive about his inexperience. Many had served for years by the time they reached Artemas's age. But Egypt had been at peace all his and Artemas's lives. It was hard to gain experience in warfare without war.

"In Alexandria's library I have studied Alexander the Great's every move, studied maps, strategies, even the words of his generals." Artemas jammed his fists onto his hips and puffed out his chest. "Experience isn't everything. But if it's experience you are looking for, you'll have it with Damon as your ship's physician."

Damon pulled Artemas by the arm. "Come on, Artemas. There'll be other ships heading to Caesar's legions."

Artemas stood rooted. Damon glanced from Artemas to the Roman captain. He could see the captain calculating how many dead oarsmen he had been forced to toss over the side on the journey here. The captain was thinking perhaps it would not be such a bad idea to take a physician aboard, protect his investment. What had Artemas gotten him into?

The captain's expressions changed as he thought this through. It was rather a slow process. Damon knew that Artemas was growing impatient. Before Artemas could say more, Damon turned to leave, hoping his friend would follow.

The captain shouted after him, "You'll not see another vessel this way for months. If it's to Caesar's forces you are headed, it's my ship or none." He pointed to Damon. "I'll take you, if you wish."

Damon yanked on the immobile Artemas. "It's both of us or none." They'd find some way to get to his father. He didn't like the looks of this captain or his rot-wormed ship.

"I suppose I could use someone to keep the latrines empty."

Damon was horrified. He pulled harder on Artemas. But Artemas broke into a grin.

"We're headed for Caesar." Artemas pinned Damon's arms to his sides in a hug and quickly added, "And to your father, too!"

"You can't be serious, Artemas."

"I'd wade barefoot in fouled bilge water if I had to. What's emptying a few buckets? Think of it, Damon. Caesar!"

# SEVEN

Damon and Artemas sat in the courtyard ripping linen sheets into narrow lengths. Mounds of strips coiled at their feet.

"I sold the last of the Venetian glass this morning," Damon said. "It didn't bring what I had hoped, but with the money we had saved for her embalming, we will have enough to last a year." Damon slit the linen with his knife and ripped another strip from the fabric.

Artemas reached for the end of a strip and began to roll. "My father borrowed a trunk for us from the retired merchant who lives next door. He had to sit through an afternoon of sea tales he'd heard a dozen times before to get it. He'll be walking the long way to market for weeks to avoid the fellow." Artemas grinned.

"How is your father taking your leaving?" Damon asked.

"I think he wishes he could come with us. Sometimes it must feel as though the vineyards have him shackled to the land."

"It must be nice to have a father who will miss you."

Artemas nodded and changed the subject. "Have you rented your house?"

"Not yet. You're sure your father doesn't mind keeping watch over my house?" The word *my* felt strange on Damon's tongue. His mother's house was now his own. He should sell it, he knew. It was much too big for one person—and the memories . . . But he wasn't ready to give it up. Perhaps when he returned.

"I think he fancies playing landlord," Artemas said. "Don't worry about my father; this suits him."

"What's left to do, then?" Damon looked down at the linen. "Besides her funeral, I mean."

"The ship sails in four days. Can you be ready? I mean, will she . . ."

"I'll be ready. Last night I finished copying the spells I think she would have chosen from the Book of the Dead. I've written all thirty-six denials on the scroll."

"Denials?"

"Before the judges she must deny having sinned. The judges have names like Breaker of Bones and Eater of Blood."

"They sound charming." Artemas reached

behind a bolt of linen. "I brought these for her."
He handed the small wooden statues of a man
and a woman to Damon.

"Why, these are shabti. What's a Greek like
you doing with these? I thought you didn't
believe in this stuff."

Artemas shrugged. "*She* did. I thought she
should have someone to help her out—you
know, where she's going."

Damon turned the shabti over in his hands.
The wood felt waxy, it was so smooth. Did he
believe? Would these wooden people become
the answerers to the gods' requests? Servants to
his mother in the afterworld? Artemas was right.
It didn't matter what he believed. "I'm glad you
thought of it. I'd hate to think of my mother
toiling in the fields for the gods because I had
forgotten to provide her with servants."

Artemas stacked another linen roll into the
papyrus basket. "She was good to me when my
mother died. She was like a second mother. If the
afterlife is what she said, soon our mothers will
be gossiping together once again." He picked up
another strip and rolled. "This seems like a lot of
linen."

Damon looked around him, at the basket
stacked with rolls and the mounds at his feet yet
to be rolled. "It does, doesn't it? I had no idea
how much I'd need. I guess I should get started."

Artemas was quiet while Damon tucked linen into the basket until he could fit in no more. Why couldn't he babble on now as he had before? Why was it when Damon needed quiet, Artemas went on and on, and now, when Damon could use something to distract him, Artemas was as silent as the Sphinx? "Will you thank your father for me?"

Artemas looked puzzled.

"For watching over my house while we're gone."

Artemas nodded.

There was nothing left to say. Damon looked one last time over his shoulder at Artemas and then entered his house, walking steadily toward the death chamber door.

Once inside, Damon put the basket beneath the table. He picked up the Book of the Dead papyrus and placed the scroll between his mother's ankles. It contained the spells to guide her and protect her on her journey through the underworld. Then he took a long strip of linen and began to wrap, binding her ankles, securing the scroll. When he came to the end of one linen roll, he took another from the basket.

He was surprised at how light she was. When the natron had dried her skin, he had removed the crystals from her body cavity and stuffed it with sawdust mixed with fragrant leaves, then sealed the incisions with beeswax. Over each cut he had stamped the Eye of Horus, the wadjet eye, in the beeswax to protect her. He thought of the stories she had told, remembered her voice, as he wrapped.

He felt the amulet that hung from his neck. It bore the image of Thoth, patron of the scribes. When all others were pushing him to begin work as a scribe, his mother had asked him why he wasn't happy. He had been chosen to practice the most noble of professions. He told her he wanted to study medicine instead. Wanted to study at the Museum. Would it anger the gods to want more when he had so much already? She had told him that it would anger the gods only if he failed to follow the path of his heart.

That night she gave him the amulet. A tiny figure of Thoth, the god of wisdom, who had given Egypt the gifts of medicine, writing, and mathematics. Damon wore it next to his heart always.

Now he lifted it over his head and placed it over her heart. "May he share your journey as he has mine, Mother."

Damon continued to wrap, round and round, until Thoth could no longer be seen.

When the body of his mother was completely covered with layers and layers of linen strips, he slid it into a linen bag, which he tied with the last few strips. In a bowl he mixed dirt from her garden with rainwater. When the mud was thick, he molded it into a ball and pressed it onto the last knot. He stamped the mud with the family seal.

"I hope this pleases you, Anubis. I have done my best. Watch over her on her journey."

# EIGHT

Damon held one end of the trunk, Artemas the other, as they made their way carefully along the dock. The harbor was crowded with ships. But as the Roman captain had predicted, not one other was departing for Spain.

Artemas inhaled deeply. "Smell it, Damon, smell the sea. It's a powerful smell."

Damon sniffed the air, but all he smelled was decaying fish and rotting seaweed. He didn't want to spoil Artemas's excitement, so he smiled and nodded. It *was* a powerful smell. He'd give Artemas that. While Artemas shielded his eyes to observe the gleaming white marble of the Pharos lighthouse, Damon pretended to wipe his nose and breathed deep the oil of lotus blossom he had applied to the back of his hand.

"What have you put in this trunk—rocks?"

Artemas adjusted his grip, his palm red and lined from the woven papyrus handle.

"Fruit. Sailors suffer from all sorts of maladies from lack of it."

"Damon, we won't be at sea more than a few weeks . . . if the yearly winds don't blow against us."

Damon looked at the Roman galley in the harbor. Even a few days aboard would be a long time. Leave it to Artemas to pick the only merchant vessel built like a warship. Why couldn't they sail on the grain run to Rome and pick up passage to Spain from there? Look at that cargo ship! It would be like sailing on an island, it was so huge.

Damon sighed. Well, at least their small galley ship would have to follow the coastline and put ashore each night. Damon found comfort in the thought of never leaving sight of land. But still, the galley looked so small.

The same boy they had seen when they arranged passage was sitting on the dock by a line to the dory. When he saw Damon and Artemas approach, he jumped to his feet, rushed forward, and took Damon's end of the trunk. He tried to lift it himself, but it was too heavy, and he nearly fell over backward trying to balance it on his chest. Artemas shook his head and pointed to the painter. The boy understood, dropped the trunk, and ran to untie the line.

Damon cringed at the *thump* the trunk made on the dock. He had packed the cooking pots inside their clothing, but still he pictured them cracked and useless.

"Just wait until you get on board." Artemas dragged the trunk, oblivious to the *thump, thump* as it crossed each gap in the cedar planks. "You'll sleep like a baby with the sea's gentle rocking."

"Good," Damon said. "I didn't sleep at all last night. I don't know if it was worry about the voyage or the hooting of the owl in my mother's garden. I found myself lying there waiting for the next hoot. Then I counted between hoots to see if they were regular, like a heartbeat, or unpredictable, like the weather." Damon studied the sky. It was clear from horizon to horizon.

Artemas scowled at Damon and shook his finger. What now? Damon looked behind him to see what was distressing Artemas.

"Not a word of night birds," Artemas scolded him. "Especially owls. No sneezing either. Sailors are more superstitious than the priests at Karnak. If you want to sail, not a word."

"What's so bad about an owl?" Damon asked.

"To a sailor it means shipwreck."

Damon snorted and shook his head. But when he stepped into the rocking dory after the trunk had been loaded, he looked again at the grain ship and wished once more for the bulk of that ship under his feet.

When the dip of the oars brought them alongside the galley, Artemas tied their trunk to the line the sailors tossed out. The captain leaned over the rail, watching his men hoist the trunk to the deck. Damon and Artemas climbed the ladder alongside the rising trunk.

The captain nudged his gubernator, and said, "He's going to save us from pirates, that one."

The sailing master tilted his head back and laughed. When he opened his mouth wide to laugh, there was a black hole on the side where teeth once had been.

"I think we'll call him the admiral." The captain jerked his head to the men carrying buckets of bilge water from the hold. They tipped the buckets over the side, the filthy water cascading down onto Artemas and Damon, who clung to the ladder. The gubernator laughed harder still.

Damon and Artemas scrambled up the ladder. Damon had one leg over the side when he saw their trunk disappearing down a hatch. "Where are they taking our trunk?" he asked Artemas.

The captain answered. "Just inspecting the contents. I'll return it to you once I'm done with it."

*Once he's taken everything of value,* Damon thought. "We packed fresh fruit, food for our passage. What will we eat?"

"Not to worry. No one starves on this ship."

The gubernator stopped laughing and eyed the rigging as if he had never seen it before.

Damon wanted to demand the trunk be brought to him, but he knew that the captain was not used to being questioned, and suddenly he was afraid to push the man any further. Was it too late to get off this ship?

Damon patted his side, thankful he'd kept at least one pouch of gold out of the trunk. He caught the captain watching him and pretended to be brushing away the oily black sediment that clung to his tunic. A few weeks, Artemas had said. Damon would be glad when they reached Spain.

The boy who had rowed them to the galley disappeared down the hatch after the trunk. He ducked quickly when the captain turned to see what Artemas and Damon were staring at. Seeing nothing but vacant deck, the captain turned to ready the ship for exit from the harbor, calling back over his shoulder, "If we need military advice, we'll be sure to shout. Oh, that's right, there's no library on this ship. What will we do?" He slapped both of his own cheeks in mock dismay.

The gubernator laughed again and saluted Artemas. "To the paper admiral!" He turned and followed the captain to the pilothouse, leaving Damon and Artemas alone on the deck.

Damon expected Artemas to be furious. He

was surprised when Artemas clapped him on the shoulder. "Think of it, Damon, we'll be at sea by midday!"

"How can you be cheerful? He's got everything." Damon didn't dare even whisper, "Except the gold at my side."

Artemas shrugged. "We'll get by. The important thing is, we are heading for your father."

*Caesar, you mean*, Damon thought. *We're headed to Caesar.* But his friend's excitement was catching . . . at least a bit. Maybe the captain would return their clothes and cooking pots. They'd be of no use to him.

Damon felt a tug at his sleeve. The boy stood close behind him. How had he snuck up on him like that? The creaking of the ship masked all other sound, Damon realized.

The boy opened a pouch. Damon recognized the pouch, but Artemas peered inside. "Our gold!"

Damon studied the boy's face. The boy looked over his shoulders, first right then left, and put the pouch in Damon's hand.

"Thank you."

The boy stayed, looking from Artemas to Damon.

"Give him a piece of gold," Artemas said.

"What? It's *our* gold." Damon frowned.

"It would be the captain's gold if he hadn't taken a hand."

"But—"

"There's a custom—if a ship is sure to go down, the crew and passengers hang gold from their necks. They hope that when a body washes ashore, whoever discovers it will be grateful for the gold and use a portion of it to see to a decent burial. The boy risked his life, I would wager, to bring us this gold. He should get something."

Damon plucked a coin from the pouch and pressed it into the boy's hand. The boy snatched it and disappeared as quickly as the smile that flickered across his face.

# NINE

Damon rested his head on the rail and closed his eyes, but it just made the nausea worse. The boat rocked, and with it his stomach surged. He threw up over the rail into the sea.

Artemas patted his shoulder. "You're lucky it's so calm. It will pass."

"I've been sick for three days. I need to get on solid land." Damon tried not to whine, but failed. "I thought we had to stick to the coastline."

"The captain decided to make a run for it. We'll save weeks by crossing open water. Be thankful you're not an oarsman in the hold."

Damon had passed the open hatches and smelled the foul fumes of human sweat and excrement from below. Just the memory of the stench made him clutch his stomach.

"We'll see land soon," Artemas assured him.

Damon threw up. He held his chalky forehead in his hand. It felt cold yet sweaty. "How soon?"

Artemas didn't answer him. Damon lifted his head.

Artemas pointed to his vomit floating. The patch of froth swirled outward.

"Can you throw up again?"

"You must be joking. I thought two days ago my stomach had to be empty. If there was anything left, it would be on your feet."

"Look. Look how it arcs away from the boat."

"So?"

"Are you sure you can't vomit again?" Artemas looked around the deck. "Never mind. Help me find something to throw overboard that floats."

Damon looked around. The rocking deck made him run for the side again. He vomited. "Happy?"

Artemas studied the vomit swirling outward. "Quick! We must tell the captain."

"I doubt he's going to have much sympathy for my seasickness."

"Not about your seasickness. The vortex."

"What?"

"We are nearing a whirlpool. We have to change course."

"Artemas, I don't mean to suggest that I don't believe you, but you've never even been out to sea before. Don't you think maybe—"

Artemas grabbed a deckhand by the shoulder. "Where's the captain? Quickly."

The deckhand pointed his chin toward the hatch. "He's in his quarters. But I wouldn't disturb him—he's sleeping."

Artemas pushed past the sailor and slid down the ladder, feet on both sides, ignoring the rungs. Damon followed, stepping carefully. "Artemas, maybe we shouldn't wake the captain."

Artemas ran toward the captain's quarters shouting, "Captain!"

The captain, stretched out in his hammock, lifted his head. "Who's making all this noise? Oh, it's you. I should have known. Go away."

Artemas grabbed the edge of the captain's hammock. "We are coming up on a whirlpool. You have to change course."

"Now, how would you know that?"

"I can see it in what floats."

The captain looked at the gubernator, who had rushed in behind Artemas and Damon. "Anything up ahead?"

The sailing master shook his head, smirking at Artemas. "The paper admiral must be studying too hard. His head is spinning."

"Then let me get some sleep, by Jove."

Artemas tried to tip the captain from his hammock. "We will all drown!"

The captain pushed Artemas away. "If he

doesn't shut up, throw him overboard." He winked at the gubernator. "Observe how he floats."

Artemas turned and ran smack into Damon. "Quick." He grabbed Damon by the upper arm and dragged him to the ladder. Damon's feet barely brushed the floor.

"Where are we going?"

Artemas pushed Damon up the rungs. When Damon lost his footing, Artemas shouldered him upward and kept climbing. Damon struggled to regain his footing and climbed faster.

The gubernator stood at the bottom, his hands on his hips. "If you see a pirate ship, Admiral," he called after them, "be sure to come back. We'll need an expert to hold our hands!"

Artemas shouted at Damon, pushing him quickly toward the stern. "The gangplank is on the deck. Throw it overboard and jump."

"But we're in the middle of the sea." Damon looked around, nothing but water full circle. "We'll need food and water."

"There isn't time."

"We'll die of thirst before we reach land."

"We'll die for sure if we stay on this boat."

"But the oarsmen? They can row."

"By the time they feel the pull of the whirlpool, the oarsmen will be useless. Hurry! It may already be too late."

"You're a madman if you think I'm going to jump off this boat into the water." Damon stood with his fists planted on his hipbones. "How can you even be sure we are headed for a vortex?"

"I've read about them. You've got to trust me!"

Damon heard the edge of hysteria in Artemas's voice. Could he be right? But jump in? Here? In the middle of nowhere? Damon shook his head and backed up a step.

"Damon, we've got to move. There's no time!"

He'd heard Artemas say those words before, with that same sound of desperation. They had been little then. The others had laughed. But Damon had trusted Artemas, and they had paddled furiously. Damon had felt silly, paddling in a frenzy when the water of the Nile was so calm, the others laughing at them. But he had done it because he had trusted his friend. The hippos had surfaced just as Artemas had predicted. Damon and Artemas had watched their friends' papyrus boats capsize. Watched the crocodiles slide from the bank into the water.

Damon closed his eyes. Artemas had been right then. Was he right again now?

Suddenly, the ship's wooden hull screeched in pain, twisted by the currents below. It shrieked as board rubbed against board.

Damon ran to help Artemas pick up the loading gangplank. It was oversized for carts, and solidly built. They strained under its weight. They lifted one end until it rested on the rail, then pushed, sliding it until it teetered in the middle.

"You!" The gubernator scrambled out of the hold.

Artemas struggled to lift the end of the plank over his head. The weight favored the half out over the water, and the plank spilled over the side, making a loud crack when it hit against the hull on its way down.

"Jump!"

Artemas was running for the edge when the boy peered out from where he was hiding behind the folded mizzen sail. The boy's eyes showed mostly white, his mouth wide. Artemas ran back and grabbed the boy, who began to kick and flail his arms. Artemas threw him overboard, then jumped after him.

Damon watched, frozen by the rail. He looked back at the gubernator hurtling toward him, screaming and turning brighter red the closer he got. Damon hated the damn boat anyhow. He vaulted over the side.

# TEN

Damon hit the water sideways. The slap stung, and he sank into the cold, cold sea. Then he stopped, suspended a moment in a flurry of bubbles before starting to rise. He broke the surface, gasping for breath and turning himself around in a circle in the water, puffing through his mouth against the cold.

The gubernator leaned over the stern, shouting and shaking a fist. Damon kept spinning, turning just in time to put his hands out and catch the gangplank in the current rushing toward him. Artemas was swimming. The boy trailed behind him, punching the water where Artemas had just been.

"Get up, use it like a raft." Artemas put both hands on the side of the gangplank and kicked his way up until his elbows were locked, then threw one leg over and rolled onto the plank. He stuck an arm out to the boy. Screaming curses, the boy tried to pull Artemas off. Artemas kicked him in the jaw. The boy's head lolled to one side, and he bobbed backward, floating away from the raft.

"What did you do that for?" Damon asked, clawing his way up onto the gangplank.

"There wasn't time for explanations, even if we could make him understand." Artemas grabbed the boy by his tunic and pulled him next to the plank. Damon hooked his arm under one of the boy's arms and Artemas hooked his under the other. Together they hauled the unconscious boy onto the plank.

Damon looked back at the ship, sailing on. The distance grew rapidly. What if Artemas was wrong? What if this was just some ocean current?

"Let's go!" Artemas screamed and madly thrashed at the water. Damon turned onto his stomach and struck out with cupped hands. They made headway against the current, but just bare-ly. It seemed as if they were standing still. Damon's shoulders began to ache, but still he beat the water as fast as he could. He gritted his teeth against the pain and pressed his chin into the gangplank. The salt stung his eyes.

The boy moved on the plank ahead of him. If he rolled off, they would have to leave him behind. They couldn't go back now. The pull was too strong. If this was a vortex, they were being sucked right into it.

"Faster!" Artemas yelled again. His voice sounded as if he were in agony. Damon counted in his head. *One, two, three, four.* The aching in his arms felt as if it were spreading. *Eight, nine, ten.* His breath was coming in short gasps now. His breath was coming so quickly he timed the strokes to it. *Twenty, twenty-one.*

He looked over his shoulder again. The ship was turning oddly now, arcing to the right. He was sure his arms would fall off if he had to take another stroke. He looked ahead at Artemas, the muscles in his back straining against the water, his head raised, water white with froth from his striking, the sea rising up all around him. Damon didn't know how much longer he could keep going. He was losing sensation in his arms. What if they couldn't escape the pull?

# ELEVEN

**D**amon felt a sudden lurch. Were they moving forward? Yes. They were skimming the calm water, moving quickly now as if they had been shot from a bow.

Damon collapsed against the board. He felt his jagged breathing, his heart pounding in his chest. In front of him Artemas still slashed wildly at the water.

"Artemas. Artemas! Stop. You can stop."

Artemas rolled onto his back and folded his arms across his heaving chest.

They watched the Roman galley. It was arcing more tightly now. The oars suddenly thrust from the sides. The galley looked like a centipede rolled on its back, thrashing at the air. The oars slapped the sea randomly. Some oars never appeared, and others fell unmanned after a few swipes—not the even rowing that Damon had seen when they had left the harbor.

The ship began to pick up speed, turning full circle, careening to one side. Damon could hear screams, or did he just imagine it? Oarsmen swarmed the deck, throwing themselves overboard, only to be swept around, then sucked under. The ship made one final turn, then tipped, holding for a heartbeat before disappearing from view as if Poseidon himself had snatched it from below.

The boy, raised up on his elbow now, stared at the spot where his ship had just been. The horizon was empty. Empty of ship, empty of men, empty of debris. Just the smooth sea in all directions.

Damon knew they had escaped the vortex, but for what? To die of thirst, with nothing but water no matter where they looked? In the dissection rooms at the Museum he had seen bodies of those who had died this way: tongues swollen to ten times their size, skin blistered from exposure. Would it have been better to have gone down with the ship? Artemas and the boy looked happy to have survived. Was Damon the only one who could see beyond the moment?

"Where do you suppose we are?" he asked. He knew Artemas had been studying charts while he, Damon, threw up over the rail during those days at sea. "Are we near land?"

"We're three days' sail from Sicily, I think. I'll know better tonight, if it's clear enough to see the stars. Not close to land, I'm afraid."

"On a trade route?" Damon imagined that enormous grain ship appearing over the horizon.

"The captain took a rather unusual route." Artemas looked down.

"No rescue, then."

"No rescue."

Damon pointed to the boy. "How are we going to tell him?"

The boy watched them speak, looking at Damon's mouth, then Artemas's, following the movement of their lips as if it would help him decipher their words.

"Tell him what?"

"That we're going to die out here."

"You don't know that."

"Oh, come on, Artemas. Look around you."

"We'll paddle to land. We can make it."

"He has a right to know," Damon said stubbornly.

"Why?"

"What if he has gods to make peace with?"

"You just want everyone to be miserable."

"We're in the middle of the sea, Artemas. We're supposed to be miserable! I wish you'd never seen the vortex. At least we'd have gone down quickly."

"It's right over there." Artemas gestured. "No one's stopping you."

Damon was so angry he felt like plunging in and swimming toward the spot where they'd last seen the ship. Any fool could see it wouldn't make a difference. One way or the other they were going to die, even if Artemas didn't want to face it. They were going to die.

# TWELVE

**D**amon's tongue filled his whole mouth. It stuck to the roof and the sides, making him gag when he tried to swallow. His throat ached for water. And he was cold. The cold made him tired. The water sucked the warmth from him, while the salt in the water sucked out the moisture. The sea was pulling the life from him.

The boy had stared numbly when the ship first went down. Then he had surprised Damon by flopping into the water on his back, spouting like a whale, and kicking his heels. Damon thought the boy had lost his mind until Artemas pointed to the scars zigzagging across his shoulders, chest, and back. He'd been whipped. Some of the scars were old, but many were fresh. In the water the boy was celebrating his captain's fate, unaware, yet, of his own.

Damon wondered what the boy felt now. At first they had paddled toward what they thought might be the nearest coast. Artemas had seemed so sure of himself. Sure they would reach land in three days. But they hadn't. And when the fourth day came and went, so did their hope of ever seeing land again. Even Artemas had stopped encouraging them, pushing them forward. Now, weak from hunger and thirst—*tortured* by thirst—they sprawled along the plank, letting the waves toss them wherever.

Damon would have cursed Artemas if it weren't so painful to talk. It was Artemas's fault that they were on this journey in the first place. Damon had wanted to send word to his father, not travel across the sea. He was a physician, not some adventurer. What had he been thinking? He had let himself get caught up in Artemas's crazy ideas. What had happened to his life since he started listening to Artemas? He had embalmed his own mother. Taken off in a galley falling apart from rot-worm. Jumped right into the middle of the sea. All to find some man who called himself Damon's father. Well, it didn't matter anymore. Nothing mattered.

Damon didn't let his arms and legs dangle over the side as the others did. He wanted the sun's warmth, but each time he felt some relief, some heat on the surface of his skin, the waves splashed over him, erasing all warmth before it had time to penetrate. He felt cold to his bones. If it weren't for the cold, Damon would have slipped over the side and let the water cover him, ending this torture. But it was so cold.

The boy rolled off the plank. He gulped the water, splashing it over his head.

Artemas yelled in Greek, "Don't drink it, the salt . . ." But his voice cracked, and his words were garbled from a tongue too thick to form sounds. Even if the boy could speak Greek, Damon wondered if he would have been able to make out those words. Maybe he knew and didn't care. Maybe he wanted the salt to draw the last bit of water from his body.

The boy splashed the water over his head, rubbing it into his scalp. Damon watched, huddled on the plank, shivering in spasms. The boy looked at Damon, his face melting into confusion.

Damon rose up on one elbow, just as the boy was thrust out of the water. He rose up to his thighs and was pushed forward at a terrific speed. Just before colliding with the plank, the boy tipped sideways, and Damon saw the white belly of a shark rolling under the plank. The shark went down, dragging the boy with him. Blood gushed upward and spread, inking the water around them. Damon and Artemas scanned the water frantically. Where was he?

The boy popped to the surface, bobbing in the middle of the circle of blood.

Artemas was the first to move. He reached out. The boy spread both hands, stretching toward Artemas. Their fingers nearly touched when the boy was snapped to one side, then jerked back again, tossed from side to side. He screamed, and blood spurted from his mouth, spraying Artemas. The red water boiled from the frenzied thrashings. Artemas thrust out one foot, kicking the shark in the snout.

The water stilled, and the boy drifted toward the plank. Artemas grabbed hold of his arm just as his face slipped below the surface. Damon helped Artemas pull him gently to the plank. They had him halfway out of the water when he was hit again with a force that knocked Damon off the plank. Damon clung to the boy's arm, but his grip slipped to the boy's wrist from the slickness of the blood. The boy was yanked from him. Damon treaded water, spinning round. The boy was gone.

"Damon, in the name of Apollo, get out of the water!" Artemas's scream came out choked and muffled by the dryness of his mouth.

Damon swam back to the plank. He was shaking so badly he couldn't pull himself up. Artemas grabbed him and rolled him onto the plank. They lay there staring at the water in disbelief.

"Did you see that? Did you see?" Artemas said,

not taking his eyes off the spot where they had last seen the boy.

"It happened so fast," Damon said.

The gangplank that had seemed so cumbersome when they were trying to push it off the deck now seemed flimsy to Damon, barely wide enough to keep their bodies out of the sea. Lying straight, he flattened his arms against his sides and held his thighs tight together, compressing himself into the center. "Do you think it'll come back?"

Artemas didn't have to say anything. Damon knew by the look on his face that it already had. He turned. The fin was knifing through the water, headed right toward the gangplank. Just when Damon was sure the shark would topple them, the fin slid below the surface. Damon saw the shadow pass under the plank. He held his breath. He could hear his heart hammering in his ears. Two more fins rose from the black water, this time so high they created a wake. Just before reaching the plank, they veered off, one to each side.

"There's more than one." Damon picked through his words carefully, his voice sounding strange even so, as though he had stuffed his mouth with cotton and was trying to talk around it.

"It's the smell of blood drawing them."

"By the gods, Artemas, look at the shadows beneath us. There must be a hundred of them."

"Too bad they smell the blood and not the lavender."

What was Artemas talking about? Damon had read that madness is often preceded by odors. He was sure that Artemas had gone mad. Then he smelled the lavender, too. Were they both insane?

# THIRTEEN

Four ships sailed right toward them. The serpents adorning the prows rose and fell with the waves. Damon closed his eyes and rubbed them with his fists. Was he hallucinating? And the smell of lavender, stronger now. Was he mad?

Artemas spoke first. "We've got to get their attention. They could sail right by without even seeing us if we just lie here."

"How many ships do you see?"

"Something wrong with your eyes? Four."

*Then they must be real,* Damon thought. Both of them couldn't be having the same hallucination. "How can we hail them?"

"I'll have to stand up and wave my arms."

"Are you crazy? If you fall off—" A shark bumped into the gangplank, jerking it sideways. The sharks seemed to be waiting, circling below. Every so often one would venture close and nose the gangplank, testing, then thrash off to one side. Angered, it seemed. Or frustrated.

"We can't just let them sail on by. They're our only hope." Artemas squatted, balancing for a moment on the balls of his feet, his fingers splayed, supporting half his weight. He straightened his knees, keeping his fingertips in contact with the wood. A wave gently raised and lowered the plank. Artemas teetered, then centered his weight and stood up, spreading his arms wide for balance. He waved his arms over his head, crossing them, then bringing them down.

Damon watched the water. The sharks seemed to back off a bit, gauging this new movement. Then one swung away from the others and darted for the plank. "Artemas, hold on!"

Artemas dropped to his knees. The shark hit the plank. It spun. Artemas flattened himself on the gangplank, but still he tipped wildly back and forth. Damon clung to the board, trying to steady it.

"We'll both go in!" Damon screamed. But the gangplank finally stopped tilting. Damon took a deep breath and held it.

The ships drew closer. Damon could see people on deck. Could they see him? Had they seen Artemas?

"I'm going to try it once more," Artemas said.

"Wait till they're closer."

"What if they change course? I have to do it now." Artemas stayed flat until there were no fins in sight, then inched his way to a crouch again.

Damon watched the shadows pass beneath him.

Artemas stood, waving his arms and shouting, "Here! Look, here! Help!" His voice was creaky but gained strength.

Damon saw a man on the lead ship point at them. "They see us, Artemas. They see us!"

A wave tossed the plank. Artemas's arms windmilled. Damon watched helplessly as his friend's weight shifted backward. His arms flailed faster, in large circles. He was going to fall in!

Artemas was thrown backward. Just as his feet lifted into the air, a shark rammed the plank, sending it gliding under him. He fell hard on his backside on the edge of the plank. Damon thought the whole plank would tip. It arched sideways, poised on the brink of turning over. Artemas strained forward to keep from falling into the water. Damon dared not grab for him but threw all his weight to the high side of the plank. It hung there, then sloshed back into the water.

The two lay head to head, panting. The shark nosed the plank, then twisted sideways, its tail skimming the surface, splashing both of them.

"As Osiris is witness, that was close." Artemas's knuckles were white from gripping the plank, but still he could not let go. "He thought he was getting dinner."

"I thought the same thing." Damon's teeth rattled from the chill. He clamped his jaw shut and rested his forehead on the plank. The surge of strength he had felt the moment when he thought Artemas would fall in drained away from him as quickly as water sinks in the desert sands. He lay on the board shaking, weaker than he had ever felt in his life.

# FOURTEEN

The lead ship cleaved through the water until it was near, then turned into the wind. The sail luffed, snapping rope and wood. Two men threw a ladder over the side.

Damon and Artemas paddled their plank to the ship. Shadows flitted beneath them. The closer they got to the hull, the faster they paddled. Damon dreaded dipping his hands in the water, expecting a shark to take his hand with each pull. He tried not to think. He focused on the bottom rung of the rope ladder ahead, tipping his chin upward so he couldn't see the movement in the water below. But he knew they were waiting. He could feel it.

When the plank thudded, wood on wood, against the ship, Damon felt the vibration through his whole body.

Artemas climbed the ladder with ease, one

hand over the other. But all Damon could do was cling to it while the sailors hauled him up. The cold, the exhaustion, the relief—all seemed to come over him at once, and he wasn't sure he could even hold on, he felt so weak. When he neared the rail, several hands grabbed him and pulled him over. He fell in a heap at the sailors' feet.

Someone wrapped a scratchy wool blanket around his shoulders. Nothing had ever felt so good.

They were all speaking at once. Damon just looked up at them, watching Artemas explain, when he realized they were speaking Egyptian. *Egyptian.* He sat up.

Cups of water were offered by hands stretched forward. There were so many bodies surrounding them that Damon couldn't tell whose hands he took his cup from. "Thank you."

Damon warned Artemas, "Don't drink too quickly. It will bring on cramps. Try to sip it." He fought his own impulse to gulp. He closed his eyes and let the water surround his tongue. He held it in his mouth even though his throat ached for it. He swallowed. His throat cooled.

When he opened his eyes, the sailors had dispersed. The captain stood over him, talking to Artemas. Damon heard them speaking of sharks.

A sailor came forward with warm soup. He

slipped away before Damon could thank him. Damon put his face over the bowl and breathed deeply. He couldn't smell the broth. The smell of lavender overpowered everything.

"It's in the sails," the captain said, as if reading his mind. "She soaks her sails in it."

"She?" Damon's voice was stronger now.

"Why, the Great One, Cleopatra. You didn't see her standard?"

Damon looked up at the flags fluttering at the bow of the ship. The image of Isis, Cleopatra's patron goddess, flapped in the breeze.

The crew had not gone far, Damon noticed. They kept busy nearby, tying and retying knots that needed no adjustment, keeping an eye on Artemas and Damon, listening. Damon heard the captain mention pirates and watched Artemas shake his head. Did they think pirates had sunk their ship? The Roman navy had swept the sea of the vermin years ago. Damon had heard that a few pirate ships remained. Like cockroaches, they had scurried away before the navy could stamp them out.

Damon's teeth still clattered. He huddled in the blanket, trying not to spill his broth, though it sloshed over the rim from the shake in his hands.

"What became of your ship?" the captain asked Artemas.

"A vortex caught her in a whirling trap. I tried to warn them. We barely made it ourselves."

"Did any others survive?"

Damon knew that Artemas was thinking about the boy, but Artemas shook his head.

The captain nodded. "There are many currents off the coast of Sicily. It is best to keep careful watch."

"So we are near Sicily?"

Damon pulled on his earlobe. His ears crackled from the water inside.

"About three days' sail."

Damon watched the crew. They had forgotten to look busy and were listening openly to Artemas and the captain.

"Where were you headed?"

"Spain and Caesar." Artemas straightened as if the very act of traveling toward Caesar deserved honor.

"When you are ready, the Pharaoh will want to speak with you. To hear it all, even the sharks, no doubt. The Great One is curious about everything."

The captain shouted to one of his men to trim the sail and strode off to see that his orders were carried out properly. The crew sprang up, heading off in different directions to their duties.

*You would never know Artemas had been in the water,* Damon thought. *Look how he throws off his blanket!*

*How he paces the deck!* Damon still didn't trust his legs. They quivered beneath his blanket.

Artemas crouched and whispered to Damon, "Be sure to mention your studies with the Pharaoh's physician, Olympus. I understand he and Cleopatra are close. Imagine! The Pharaoh herself."

Damon leaned his head to one side and thumped the top of his head, trying to drain the water from his ear.

"And be sure to say you're a physician. Cleopatra admires the sciences."

"Calm yourself, Artemas. I think you're more nervous now than you were with the sharks."

With mention of the sharks, both of them thought of the boy and grew silent. They sipped their broth.

# FIFTEEN

*S*he's not as beautiful as they say, Damon thought. Her hair was not silken black, as he had expected, but brown with a curl to it. And her eyes were large for her small face. Only her mouth was as he had pictured it. Her lips were full and perfectly formed, as if chiseled from stone.

"Sit, relax. Your journey has been hampered by the gods. Let it take a turn for the better now." Cleopatra welcomed them as if they were nobility, indicating piles of Persian rugs on which to recline.

Damon felt like nobility in the tunic Cleopatra's servants had provided. He'd never touched anything so soft. Could this really be happening? Lounging with a Pharaoh? He'd heard rumors that Cleopatra sometimes stole into the Museum disguised, attending lectures with the students, joining their discussions as if she were one of them. He'd never believed it. Could it be?

Or maybe he was dead. Maybe he had drowned, and this was the otherworld, where commoners and gods mingled.

Cleopatra settled onto a couch supported by four carved lions, tucking her bare feet under her. She seemed so at ease, as if every day she sat with two lowly subjects. Damon casually slid his hand under his leg and pinched it. Not dreaming.

"It is lucky for you that I found it necessary to escape the weariness of Rome for a few days, refreshing myself on the open sea."

"It is indeed our good fortune. We owe you our lives." Artemas swept an arm across his waist and bowed over it. *No, it's real,* Damon thought. *In the otherworld Artemas wouldn't act like such an ass.*

Artemas's brow furrowed. "Is Rome so dull you need escape?"

Cleopatra laughed. The music of it delighted Damon. She sounded like the wind chimes in his mother's garden. "My weariness comes not from boredom, but from having to be on guard against my enemies. It grows tedious."

"Your enemies are my enemies." Artemas bowed his head this time. Damon rolled his eyes.

"Then we had best find you a sharp sword. You will be defending me on all sides. To the

Romans I am a pagan temptress, casting spells on their beloved Caesar."

Damon had heard the Roman slander. Imagine—Caesar, who stole the wives and even the daughters of his own friends, beguiled by the innocent Cleopatra! It was she who should be careful. But Damon held his tongue.

Cleopatra rose and trimmed the wick of a wax incense cone, then lit it with the flame from another candle. "Winter is not long past. What brings you from Egypt so early in the season?"

"How did you know we sailed from Egypt?" Damon asked.

Cleopatra merely smiled, clapped her hands, and spoke in Nubian to a servant nearby. She must have requested refreshment, for the girl returned shortly bearing a tray with three cups.

Cleopatra reclined, her cup in hand, and switched from Greek to Egyptian to speak to Damon. "You must tell me news from home."

When Cleopatra mentioned home, Damon could think of nothing but the loss of his mother. He knew Cleopatra must want news of her country. The fate of one old woman could not be of interest, but he found himself telling her of his mother anyhow.

She listened intently, rising up and sitting near him when he faltered. She put a hand on his. "I shall send word to my priests to pray for her."

Damon knew that she would.

She asked Artemas in Greek, "Where are you headed?"

"To Caesar. Damon's father serves his legion. A centurion." Artemas spoke with such pride, it sounded as if he were talking about his own father. "We must bring him news of his wife's journey to the other bank."

With the mention of Caesar, Cleopatra stood, setting down her cup. She clasped her hands, squeezing and releasing her fingers. "We have heard little from Spain. He camps through the cold winter on his enemy's doorstep at Munda. They outnumber him, thirteen legions to his eight."

Artemas stood. "Eight of Caesar's legions are like twenty of any other. Mere numbers are not enough to defeat him."

Behind a row of trunks chained to the deck a curtain was strung from the rigging. The breeze billowed the sheer fabric, and Damon saw a woman waiting. Cleopatra missed nothing. She followed Damon's stare. "Charmion, come." Charmion stroked Cleopatra's arm and whispered to her.

Cleopatra squeezed Charmion's hand, then turned to Artemas and Damon. "My brother, Ptolemy, is not well. You will have to excuse me."

"May I help?" Damon pulled off the blanket draped over his shoulders. "I studied in your Museum, under Olympus."

"Olympus?" Cleopatra smiled. "I do miss him. So does Ptolemy. Yes, come. Perhaps the gods had designs when they took your ship."

Damon followed Cleopatra and Charmion through a maze of billowing fabric to where Ptolemy was stretched out across several floor pillows. Ptolemy's face was ashen, the color drained from it. Damon felt the boy's brow and, holding his wrist, found a weak pulse. "You must stop the bloodletting," he told Cleopatra. "It is weakening him." Damon knew that many believed in bleeding, but he had found no evidence that it made a patient stronger.

Ptolemy coughed. The spasms drained what little strength he had. He collapsed onto the bed when the fit passed.

"If we could get some dried fenugreek, we could burn it," Damon said. "The smoke has a soothing effect on the lungs."

Cleopatra spoke to a servant in Latin. Damon raised his eyebrows. It was said that she spoke a dozen languages. She had been in Rome but six months and already spoke Latin. Damon's father was Roman, and Damon could barely put six words together. He shook his head.

Cleopatra sat next to her brother, smoothing

his hair away from his forehead. "My servant will see what can be done. We are limited here on the ship, but whatever you need can be had as soon as we reach shore."

"I can make a poultice of dried figs."

"That we have, I am sure." Cleopatra nodded to Charmion, who sped away.

"He has a fever." Damon began to pull off the blanket that covered Ptolemy. Cleopatra seized his arm to stop him. Damon was surprised by her strength. He hadn't expected it. She was so small and slight.

"Will the chill not make him worse?" Cleopatra asked.

"Feel him. He is hot. Does it make sense to trap the heat inside?"

She didn't answer him. He knew that many physicians wrapped their patients like mummies when they suffered the burning sickness. But Damon knew Olympus would not.

Damon was aware that Cleopatra didn't trust him. What must it be like to trust no one? To be always on guard? He folded the blanket back. She didn't stop him this time, but he felt her eyes on him. She would watch him closely, he knew. He began the healing chants. He didn't believe they helped, but they would do no harm, and he needed something to take his mind off the Pharaoh, Cleopatra, so close beside him.

# SIXTEEN

By the time the port of Ostia came into view, Ptolemy's fever had broken and his lungs had cleared a bit. His color had returned to normal, and he was able to sit up.

Damon joined Artemas on deck, staying close to the rail, out of the way of the sailors racing to bring down the sail. The silver-tipped oars dipped into the water, and soon a steady pull moved the ship forward. Damon timed his footing to the rhythmic swoosh of the oars, bracing himself with each lunge, gripping the rail for balance. The breeze on his face felt good, and his stomach was only mildly distressed.

The lighthouse rose up from a narrow strip of land to their left.

Cleopatra stood as sure-footed as Artemas on the heaving deck. She pointed to the lighthouse. "I prefer her sister in Alexandria."

Artemas shaded his eyes against the sun's glare off the water. "And the land, all red clay," he said. "Alexandria's brilliant white seems so clean."

Damon watched the wind lift Cleopatra's hair off her shoulders and away from her face. She *was* beautiful. How could he have not seen it before? He looked away.

"Ptolemy has improved. It seems that you have paid your debt to me."

"We can never repay you for saving us," Damon said.

Cleopatra hesitated. "There is one thing."

Damon could see the indecision in her gray eyes and the turn of her lips.

"There is a man. His name is Cicero. He speaks out against Caesar. He is very clever, and many get lost in the twisted labyrinths of his speeches."

Artemas folded his arms across his chest, oblivious to the lurching of the ship. Damon knew Artemas did not like this man Cicero, even though he had never met him. Woe to the man who spoke ill of Caesar to Artemas! Damon kept his eyes on the horizon, his stomach beginning to lurch with the ship.

"I have sent many spies." She looked out over the water, speaking softly. "They can find nothing useful."

"What is it you hope to find?" Damon swallowed hard. His stomach contents were beginning to rise to meet his tonsils.

"Proof that he is a traitor. I fear for Caesar."

"If the spies couldn't help you, how can we?" Damon asked.

"Cicero is a lawyer. My informants tell me he hires boys off the street as witnesses for his trials. Perhaps if he were to hire you, you might learn something useful. Something I might use to convince Caesar that he is dangerous."

"But we must waste no time leaving for Spain. It will take us two months over land." Damon spoke quickly, before Artemas could answer. His good-hearted friend would get them into this plot for sure.

"I will find you passage on a ship headed your way if you do this."

"I was getting accustomed to the idea of land travel." Damon struggled with his stomach. He did not want to vomit in front of Cleopatra. Wasn't it just moments ago he was beginning to enjoy the ship?

"Then I will provide you with swift horses. By horse, you could be to Caesar in a month, sooner if you travel hard."

Damon knew she could command them. Or she could find others. Cleopatra trusted them. How could they refuse their Pharaoh? He sighed. "Tell us what you want us to do."

Artemas clapped him on the back so hard he thought he would throw up all over Cleopatra's feet.

Cleopatra smiled slightly and turned to the water. "This canal leads to the Tiber."

The movement of the ship slowed and leveled out. Land was a stone's throw on either side of them. For the first time since they'd been rescued, Damon thought about his father. What if Damon didn't recognize Litigus? It had been almost six years. Without his mother to bring them together, they would be nothing more than strangers. As Damon watched the city walls slip by and listened to Artemas and Cleopatra plan their espionage, he felt a sudden longing to be back in the Museum, safely lulled by one of his professor's lectures. Artemas might thrive on adventure, but he did not.

# SEVENTEEN

**D**amon and Artemas turned right off the Via Sacra. Artemas walked backward in front of Damon saying, "But we have *hours* before court goes into session, and the Circus Maximus is not far. The gladiators—think of it, the fiercest fighters in all the world! When will we ever have the chance again?"

Damon supposed he would want to see the hospital on Tiber Island if there was time, so why did he feel so annoyed that Artemas wanted to see his foolish warriors? "Oh, all right. But we have to get to the courthouse early. The sooner we have something to report on Cicero—*anything* to report on Cicero—the sooner we can leave for Munda and my father."

Artemas bumped into a street vendor, who cursed him. Artemas just laughed and patted the man's shoulder, not the least bit upset when the man slapped his hand away.

The noise of the city made it difficult to talk. The clatter of wagon wheels on the roadways competed with the cries of vendors hawking their wares. A curtained litter shouldered by four slaves plowed through the middle of the via, forcing Artemas and Damon to one side. Behind it a flock of sheep scattered, only to be regrouped by a small dog nipping at heels and barking while darting around the rim of the closing circle. The sheep seemed alarmed by the city noises, making the dog's job that much harder. Damon and Artemas backed up against a storefront until the flock passed, then wove, single file, through the crowds that thickened as they got closer to the Circus Maximus.

The sun was hot, even this early in spring, so Artemas and Damon looked for seats under tarpaulin. They found some on the edge. The smell of caged animals and sweat bloomed in the heat. The performance had begun at sunrise, the brilliant hour, and already dozens of animal carcasses were heaped in a pile on the far side of the arena. Damon was glad they had chosen seats above the caged animals rather than above the dead ones. Even from here, when the wind was right, he could smell the rotting flesh. A cloud of flies swarmed the mound. He could see the spectators over the dead animals swatting at stray flies. Why had he allowed Artemas to talk him into coming here?

Artemas leaned forward, his elbows resting on his knees, his fingers locked together.

From an arched doorway a man appeared.

"Damon, look. The retiarius, the fisherman—a gladiator."

Damon only knew what Artemas was saying by watching his lips. He couldn't hear anything over the noise of the spectators, who were whistling, yelling, and stamping their feet on the wooden flooring.

The gladiator strode out into the middle of the arena, his arms raised to the cheering crowd. He appeared to be nearly unarmed. His left arm was covered with what looked like a sleeve made of metal strips that went all the way to his shoulder. He carried a long trident and a net. Perhaps this would not be so bad, after all.

Artemas leaned over and yelled into Damon's ear, "Combat between fish and fisherman!"

From an archway across the arena a murmillon stepped out—the fish. A fish carved from bone was attached to his metal helmet. He carried a sword, a javelin, and two knives at his belt. How could this be fair?

The crowd hushed as the two circled each other. The retiarius swung his net over his head, but before he could release it, the murmillon thrust his sword. The retiarius dodged, but the sword slit his leather breastplate. A thin line of blood leaked. The crowd cheered wildly. They sounded frenzied, as if they had gone mad.

Clutching his side, the fisherman warded off the attacks of the fish with his other arm. Even wounded, his skill was great. He pinned his opponent's sword with his trident and flicked it out of reach. Artemas clapped his hands and whistled. Damon felt sick. What was he doing here?

The fisherman was growing weaker, and slower. The fish had lost his sword, but he just switched to the longer javelin and pulled a knife from his belt. With the javelin, the fish twisted the trident up and back and moved in close to the defenseless fisherman. He plunged his knife into the fisherman's side. The fisherman fell forward onto his knees, his face in the dirt. The murmillon stood over him. The crowd's crazed cheers formed a chant. Although Damon heard one or two weak shouts of *"Mitte"* to save the life of the wounded retiarius, the crowd's chant grew into a crescendo of *"Iugula,"* and the fish, bowing to the crowd's demands, slit the fisherman's throat. How could Artemas consider this entertainment? Damon glared at him. Artemas stared straight ahead.

Damon looked over his shoulder, scanning the crowd. They all clapped and whistled, many jumping from their seats to watch the dead gladiator being dragged out of the arena. This was supposed to be the center of the civilized world?

Artemas still leaned forward. But his shoulders sagged, and he no longer cheered. He rubbed his hands together, over and over.

Damon punched his shoulder. "Is this what you wanted to see?"

Artemas didn't turn.

Damon hit him again. "Brave warriors! Illustrious combat! Is this what you want to be? Take a good look. This is what it looks like for one man to kill another."

Through clenched teeth Artemas said, "This isn't what I want to be."

Damon had had enough. But before he could suggest they leave, a lone juggler walked to the center of the arena, tossing five flaming clubs high in the air. Her head was tipped back to follow the clubs, so from where they sat, Damon and Artemas could see her young face locked in concentration. Her hair was loose and flowed down over her shoulders in spirals. Damon released a deep breath. They would watch the juggler. He would take deep breaths and get rid of his anger. Then they would leave.

The crowd laughed when the juggler had to reach out far to catch a club that strayed from its normal path. She struggled to regain the steady flow of clubs. After a moment or two of teetering, she had them back under control and spun around, catching them behind her back. A flickering of applause scattered through the audience.

Damon was so mesmerized by the tilt of her chin and the flow of the torches that until Artemas tensed he noticed nothing in the ring but the juggler. The rhinoceros seemed to come out of nowhere, as if it rose from the floor itself. It shook its head, adjusting to the bright light. Damon remembered reading that the rhinoceros is almost completely blind. But even with such poor sight, how could it miss the torches whisking in front of it? The juggler had her back to the rhinoceros, and Damon, watching the upturned face, realized with a sudden wave of nausea that the girl knew her fate. Her jaw was set as if preparing for the impact.

The rhinoceros pawed the ground with one hoof, snorting. The crowd was again frenzied. Damon rose to leave, tugging at Artemas, but Artemas pulled away. The rhinoceros dropped its head, its horn scraping the floor, and, to the increasing roar of the crowd, began to charge. Damon watched the girl close her eyes and the torches fall one by one to her feet. The horn of the rhinoceros pierced her back. The beast raised its head, and the girl, run through by the horn, was lifted off her feet. The rhinoceros trotted around in circles, tossing its head back and forth, trying to free itself of the burden. The girl, lifeless, hung from the horn, her arms and legs flopping up and down with each jerk of the beast's head.

Damon turned his back to the arena. A group behind him stood, waving him to sit so they could see. They yelled, but he stared over their heads. Damon looked from Artemas to the crowd to the arena. He pressed his palms to his ears, hard. But the mad roar of the crowd penetrated. Penetrated everything.

Artemas spit on the ground of the Circus and half ran out, leaving Damon to follow as best he could. The crowd didn't part when they saw Damon coming, and he had trouble wedging himself between the spectators.

The cheering reached another pitch, and Damon, unable to help himself, looked back. The girl lay contorted in the dirt, a leg buckled under her body. And the beast was being slaughtered by a dozen armed guards whose spears had difficulty piercing its tough hide. The crowd was cheering the trampling of one guard.

Damon let Artemas get far ahead. His friend needed time alone. This wasn't what Artemas had expected. Rome was not what either of them had expected. Damon longed for the gentleness of the Egyptian people—the peace of Alexandria. He studied the contorted faces of those in the crowd. Was his father like these men? A chill passed through him, and he hurried to catch up with Artemas.

# EIGHTEEN

It was as if the bust of Cicero that stood on a pedestal in the foyer of Damon's home, back in Alexandria, had come to life on the Forum steps. The beefy, balding man with prominent nose and deep creases along his cheek and jaw so resembled the bust Damon had passed hundreds of times that the real Cicero now seemed familiar to him—as if Damon were seeing an old friend.

Cicero shrugged his cloak off one shoulder. He spoke to a man who Damon guessed was his servant, since he did not have on the toga worn by citizens of Rome. Cicero's waistband, Damon noticed, was purple, a color supposedly reserved for senators. When Cleopatra had dressed in purple to attend the theater, Cicero had criticized her at length. It seemed he paid no attention to his own words—or he thought himself worthy where Cleopatra was not.

Cicero pointed out several in the crowd to his servant, then turned and climbed the Forum steps, taking two at a time. When he reached the top step, he shouted, "A good day's wage for those who are interested. See my man, Tiro."

A crowd began to form around Tiro, who shouted, "No work required!"

A man dressed in rags shouted back, "You think it's not work to listen to those long-winded jackasses?" The crowd laughed, but still more joined the group.

"You, the one missing the foot. Yes, you." Tiro gestured to a lame man to come forward. "We're in need of your kind." Several beggars joined the group.

A legless man used his arms to swing his torso up the steps. "Worked for Cicero before. Decent man," he hollered to the crowd.

Tiro motioned to them all. "Follow me."

They followed him to a chamber in the court-house. The others seemed to leave space around Artemas, who stood a head taller, but Damon had to elbow and wedge himself through the flow of Romans, just as he had at the Circus Maximus.

Damon wondered how they would all fit into this small room. Why did Tiro need so many? The room was packed. He seemed to have favored the blind, deaf, and crippled. Would he and Artemas get picked? If they weren't chosen, how would they get close enough to Cicero to learn anything useful to the Pharaoh? Damon found himself limping, then scolded himself for the deception. He'd never make a spy. He wished he hadn't agreed to this.

Cicero entered through a side door and stood at a podium. "The case you are about to hear will be painful for many of you. Who in Rome has not suffered the landlord's greed?"

Around the room men grumbled and nodded.

"My client lived in the attic of a tenement near the cattle markets. One evening, while his family slept, the roof collapsed. The rubble caught fire from a brazier that had been lit to take off the night chill. My client had been working late. He rounded the corner to see his building in flames. His whole family burned to death. His and many others." Cicero swept back his cloak. "They were killed because the landlord had hired an architect known to cut costs by using inferior materials and insufficient supports. How long are the people of Rome going to stand for this shoddy construction that takes the lives of our people?"

The grumbling grew louder. The man next to Damon thumped his crutch on the floor. Even Damon found himself swept up in the passion of Cicero's speech. *How dare the wealthy get richer at the cost of human life?*

"Will you join me in battle against them?"

The group shouted agreement. Damon joined them, raising a fist and shouting, "We are with you." Artemas glared at him.

"Good. I want the jury to see how high rents force ten into a space meant for two. I want them to understand that when a building crumbles, hundreds are injured and homeless. You will show them. You will fill the galleries. Together we will put a stop to the human sacrifice. Are we one?"

"Yes!"

"Many of you already have afflictions. Good. Those of you who need a little something extra, see Tiro. He will provide you with bandages and crutches."

What? What was this? Had Damon heard right? He looked to where Cicero had gestured. Tiro stood behind a pile of soiled bandages. A dozen crutches leaned against the wall behind him.

Cicero raised his fist. "You are crusaders against injustice!"

How had he let himself be fooled so easily? Cicero didn't care about the poor. Damon whispered to Artemas, "I'll not put on some filthy bandage and pretend I've been injured."

"But how else do you expect to get close to him? You want those horses, don't you?"

"But this is all a sham!"

Artemas rolled his eyes. "What did you expect? Don't you see that this is just one way to show the jury the truth?"

Damon folded his arms across his chest. "I won't do it."

"All right, have it your way. Sitting in a courtroom for days won't really help us learn anything about Cicero anyhow." Artemas raised his hand and shouted, "Excuse me?"

"Yes, you." Cicero pointed to Artemas.

"How long do you expect this trial to last?"

Now what was Artemas up to? They'd be found out, for sure. What did the Romans do to spies? Damon thought of the Circus Maximus—the juggler—and shuddered.

"You should receive several days' pay. At least three. Those of you with natural afflictions can leave your names with Tiro. We will use you again. Crippling injuries go a long way in the courtroom." Cicero headed toward the door with a wave to the crowd.

Artemas raised his voice. "I'm afraid my friend and I can't spare that much time. We are going to Caesar, you see."

Cicero stopped midstride and turned. "Then let me speak with you before you go. Come."

Cleopatra was right, Damon thought. Cicero must be obsessed with Caesar to agree to meet with them, two young men he had never seen before.

Artemas and Damon followed Cicero through the marble corridor to a small chamber, bare except for a desk and a few chairs. Cicero was the first to speak. "There has been little news out of Spain."

"Yes, so we understand," Damon replied. "My father is there. I go to tell him of my mother's death. He serves Caesar."

"I will double the wage you would receive in the court if you send me word of how the battle goes in Spain."

Artemas stroked his chin with one hand. "What kind of news are you hoping for?"

Cicero looked sharply at Artemas. "What are you suggesting?"

"It's common knowledge you have no allegiance to Caesar. Will you use our information against him?" So, Damon thought, *Artemas is expecting an honest answer. I'd sooner believe a viper.*

"I swear allegiance to no man. My allegiance is to the Republic." Cicero put his foot up on the chair, tightening the leather straps of his sandal. "I only desire news on which way the battle goes."

Artemas kept Cicero squarely in front of him like the hunter who never turns his back on the beast. "It is said that Cleopatra has many men following Caesar's progress. Perhaps you should ask her how the battle goes."

"The Egyptian sorceress? She will be the

downfall of the Republic." Cicero was doing nothing to hide his distrust of Cleopatra—but if such thoughts were treasonous, all of Rome would be arrested. "I am a man of honor: I will not humble myself by begging that pagan for information."

Damon laughed, then coughed behind one fist to cover the sound. When both Artemas and Cicero looked at him, he asked, "How is it that a man of honor deceives a jury?"

"Ah, that." Cicero waved it away as if he were fanning an annoying insect from in front of his face. "That is merely throwing dust in the jurymen's eyes. It is the lawyer's calling."

"You are good at this?" Damon asked.

"I am the best."

"I shall remember to protect my eyes."

Cicero smiled. "Your ears as well, son. Especially your ears."

Damon could not help but smile in return. Cicero's voice was deep with resonance, soothing as a balm. How could he protect his ears against it? And something more—Cicero had called him *son*. Did he need to be someone's son so badly he was willing to be charmed by an enemy of his Pharaoh?

Artemas crossed his arms stubbornly. "I'll not betray Caesar."

Cicero shrugged. "I only ask news of the battle, no more."

Damon believed him. He knew he shouldn't. There was dust in the air, and Cicero was throwing it. But Damon knew that information was power, and the first to know could strut his importance. Cicero was someone who liked to strut, Damon was sure. This was not about Caesar—at least, not this time.

"How would we send word?" Artemas asked cautiously.

"Messenger. Tiro will supply you with funds, and extra for your trouble. Now, I'm afraid I am late for court." Cicero left without waiting for their answer. Did he read men so well that he knew they would send word? If so, he must also know they would choose those words carefully. And that first their Pharaoh, Cleopatra, would hear.

"What are we going to do?" Damon asked Artemas after Cicero had left.

"I won't provide him with so much as a breath to use against Caesar—or Cleopatra."

Damon had been ready to collect payment from Tiro and send Cicero news of progress in Munda. All because of one word—*son*. Artemas had kept his head. Cicero was not to be trusted. He was a man who created illusions. And a lie was still a lie, whether you liked to call it dust in the eyes or not.

# NINETEEN

Damon breathed deep the incense Cleopatra burned. It smelled of Egypt. It smelled of home. He missed home.

"Cicero has a voice that would charm the snake." Cleopatra clapped her hands. Charmion appeared with wine.

Damon plucked a fig from the platter of dried fruits. "He told me to protect my ears."

"And well you should."

Artemas refused the wine. "I don't trust him."

"Then you are wiser than Caesar himself." Cleopatra sent a lotus blossom, floating in a bowl, spinning with a flick of her finger. "Caesar is too forgiving. His trust will be his downfall. Did you hear what he said of Cicero? That it is better to have extended the frontiers of the mind than to have pushed back the boundaries of the Republic. He put Cicero above himself!" Cleopatra shook her head. "I owe you horses."

Artemas knelt before Cleopatra. "But we have learned nothing."

"You will have your horses." Cleopatra signaled a servant. "You found out as much as any of my paid spies. It is as I suspected. Cicero watches Caesar closely."

*The world watches Caesar closely,* Damon thought. *Why should Cicero be any different?*

Damon cleared his throat and looked at Artemas. They had agreed that Artemas should warn her of the real danger even if it angered her. Now was the time.

Artemas stood and bowed his head. "I fear you have more to fear from Cicero than Caesar does, O Great One. Cicero's dislike for you goes beyond rational thought. It seems personal. He blames you for all that is wrong with Caesar."

"Cicero can't harm me. It is Caesar I worry about."

"I thought you should know."

"I appreciate your candor. Not many would say so."

"If you don't want to give us the horses now, I would understand."

"You have earned them. Even more so with your honesty. But I do ask you one more favor."

Artemas was on one knee in an instant. "Anything, my Pharaoh."

"Take this to Caesar." She handed him a scroll,

sealed with the royal emblem. "Trust it to no one else—his hands or none."

Artemas took the scroll and held it to his heart.

Damon realized this meant Artemas would see the great Caesar himself. Artemas would ride like a man possessed. How would Damon keep up?

Cleopatra held out both hands. Cupped in the palm of each hand was a small stone. "An amulet, for your safety."

Damon felt the warmth of the stone that must have come from her own hand. The Great One's own heat. He closed his hand around the amulet and felt it radiate. He opened his hand again to study it. The small oval turquoise was carved with the Eye of Horus, the wadjet eye. He felt its protection just as surely as he had felt the heat. He bowed to Cleopatra and remained with his forehead to the limestone floor even after her scent of lavender had left the room.

# TWENTY

At the first milestone they came to, Artemas reined in his horse. The horse, energized by the early morning chill, pranced in an arc around the column. Although the distance in miles to many towns was carved into the stone, the mileage to Munda was not. Damon was glad. He knew it must be more than a thousand miles. To see that number etched in stone might make him reconsider the journey ahead.

They kept a good pace all morning. By noon they found themselves at the thirtieth-mile marker, facing the mouth of a gaping hole in the hill before them. The horses pranced backward and sidestepped.

Damon struggled to keep his mount still. "What do you make of it?" he asked Artemas.

"It must be part of the road. Look how the stones fit together. It's paved right on through."

"It's dark in there. I can't see to the other side."
Damon squinted into the darkness. "How do we
know the earth doesn't just open up, with the
Devourer waiting at the bottom?"

"The road leads here. It must go through."

Damon heard tortured creaking coming from
the mouth of the gaping hole in the earth. Had he
conjured the Devourer by speaking his name? A
dull thud, like the heartbeat of a giant beast,
came steadily. Damon's horse backed farther
away from the dark opening.

Damon was about to turn and flee when two
oxen came into the light. They slowly plodded
forward, pulling a wagon. The driver flicked a
whip back and forth in time with the beat of the
hooves on the stone.

The driver guided the oxen to a stop by the
side of the road near a statue of Mercury. The old
man climbed down from his perch and searched
the ground, prodding it with his whip handle
until he loosened a small stone. He tossed it onto
a large pile of stones in front of the statue.

The driver saluted Damon and Artemas. "You
might want to add a stone to the Mercury heap.
Protector of travelers, you know. Never hurts to
have a bit of luck."

Artemas nodded. "How goes the road ahead?"

"Never seen a tunnel, I wager."

"A tunnel?"

"Army dug right through the hill. You can't say the Romans don't build their roads straight. Paved all the way through too."

"How deep?" Damon asked.

"It doesn't go down. Just think of it as a road with a canopy." The driver pulled himself up onto the wagon. "May Mercury be at your heels." The wagon began to move.

"How far to the nearest inn?" Artemas shouted over the creaking of the wheels.

The driver cupped his hand to his ear. "Eh?"

"The nearest inn?"

"The fourth stone."

Damon and Artemas watched the man's back until he disappeared from view. Then it couldn't be avoided. They turned to the gaping hole. Damon was sure they were entering a tomb. So many lined the roads—could this be one with a gateway to the otherworld?

Artemas gathered in his horse's reins. "I'll go first. If I slip out of sight, turn and run for it. Don't worry about the horse's feet on the stone. Just go for all she's got."

Artemas entered the tunnel. Damon followed. It was dark, but he could still see the outline of Artemas in front of him. The clopping hooves echoed, making it sound as if a dozen horses had come in with them.

"I can't understand why this isn't marked on

the map." Artemas's voice boomed in the narrow space. It sounded oddly hollow, as if it were coming from the walls instead of from Artemas.

Damon's eyes began to adjust to the dim light. He could make out the walls of the tunnel and the ceiling overhead, covered in moss. He prodded his horse on with his heels to her belly, but the mare ignored him and only reluctantly moved forward. "You don't suppose that old man was . . ."

"Who?" Artemas turned to look over his shoulder, resting his hand on his horse's rump.

"Nobody." Damon shrugged. He was a man of science, by Thoth. Why was he thinking about demons? He wasn't a little boy afraid of the dark. Why did he feel like one? He'd escaped a vortex, even a shark attack. He squared his shoulders and rode on.

Light struck the sides of the tunnel. The horses picked up their pace.

The sunlight seemed brighter when they emerged. Damon and Artemas looked all around them, marveling at the light on the leaves.

"I believe I'm starving," Artemas said over his shoulder.

Damon trotted to catch up. "The next stone is up ahead, only three miles to go."

The two rode in the sunshine, hungry and tired. Damon's legs were sore. He wondered how well he would be able to walk when he finally got off his fat mare.

When they rounded a wide bend in the road, Damon saw the inn ahead. He was surprised at how crowded it appeared. Several wagons were pulled up in front.

"Must be good food here," Damon said. "It looks busy."

Artemas leaned forward. "Soldiers."

Damon and Artemas brought their horses to a stop between two chariots. Several soldiers milled around a wagon. They all wore red cloaks. The plumes on their helmets were of the same red. They were Roman.

As Artemas and Damon led their horses to the water trough, Damon smelled something all too familiar. Artemas must have smelled it, too. But either he didn't know what he was smelling or he was too taken with the soldiers to put it together. Damon suspected the latter.

"Any news from Caesar and Spain?" Artemas asked the soldier nearest him.

"The battle continues at Munda. Caesar has pushed the enemy back."

"Even outnumbered, Caesar triumphs."

"Yes, but we lost many men." The soldier pointed to the wagon. "We carry news to the magistrate, and a wounded man to his family on the way."

"My friend here is a physician," Artemas said.

"His wound worsens. The doctor in Munda dressed it, but the dressing should be changed." The soldier looked at Damon hopefully.

Damon undid his cloak and passed it to Artemas. "Certainly, I'll do what I can." He stepped forward. With each step the unmistakable odor of decaying flesh grew stronger. It overpowered even the rankness of the unwashed soldiers.

Artemas looked uneasy.

The wounded man lay on a bed of straw. Damon climbed into the open wagon next to him. The bandages were stiff with dried blood. This close, the stench was overwhelming. Damon gagged. He breathed through his mouth.

He knew what he would find when he peeled back the bandages. There was no mistaking this fetid odor. "Have you fresh bandages?"

One of the soldiers volunteered to get some from the inn.

"And water to bathe him and give him to drink," Damon called after the soldier.

The man lay feverish, tossing his head from side to side and muttering in Latin, words unfamiliar to Damon. "Could someone translate, please?"

"He calls to his wife," a soldier told Damon in Greek.

Damon clenched his jaw, breathing through

his teeth, fighting back the spasms and the bile that rose in the back of his throat. He cut the bandages free with his knife. He peeled back the cloth. A writhing mass of pale yellow maggots fell away from the rotting flesh, dropping like rice from a stalk. On the wagon floor they curled first one way and then the other, protesting the light. One soldier retched beside the wagon wheel. Another turned ashen but stayed near. Artemas fainted.

"Shall I bring your friend to?" a soldier asked Damon.

"No, leave him. It's good he fell in the brush. He'll get a few scratches, but at least he didn't crack his skull open on the road." Damon worked quickly now. "You'll need to keep the maggots in darkness."

"You're not going to remove them?"

"Most likely the physician in Munda put them there. They eat away at the dead flesh that poisons the leg. It is good."

"Not so good to look at."

"No," Damon agreed. "Not so good to look at."

The man's leg had angry red streaks up into the thigh from the wound below the knee. The flesh was gray and spongy.

"You'll need to get him to his family— quickly."

"Can't anything be done?"

"Just make him as comfortable as possible." Damon packed the maggots back into the fresh linen. "And travel with speed."

The soldiers nodded grimly. Damon knew they had expected as much.

He jumped out of the wagon. "See if you can get him to take some water."

Damon crouched beside Artemas and slapped him lightly on the cheek. Artemas rolled his head from side to side, dazed. He looked at Damon as if he were having difficulty keeping him in focus. His eyes lost their dull look, then widened. He pulled back from Damon, staring horrified at Damon's shoulder.

Damon tucked in his chin to see what Artemas was looking at, then flicked a maggot from his shoulder into the dirt. "Are you ready for some lunch?"

"I'm not very hungry," Artemas answered weakly.

"Then let's get back on the road." Damon felt a sense of urgency. What if his father were wounded like this man?

# TWENTY-ONE

They saw the smoke in the distance. Wagons piled with the dead and wounded clattered past them. At first Damon searched every soldier's face, looking for his father, but then there were too many. Now a steady stream of men flowed against them, the faces smudged with dirt.

Damon looked down at his own spattered cloak. It was stiff with mud. His legs were caked with it. His face must look like those they passed—eyes too big and sunken from lack of sleep, staring out from a black mask. His horse stumbled on a stone. The roads built by Roman soldiers had ended days ago.

Damon twisted from the waist to look back at Artemas. "We must be near."

Artemas nodded, his face grim.

Damon's aches were old from so many days on horseback. Some were so deep they were just memories of earlier pains. His hands were cal-loused from the abrasive rope reins. His buttocks were numb. He felt as if he had been beaten with a club.

Artemas cupped a hand and hollered forward to Damon. "Look ahead. A standard."

A pole rose from behind an outcropping far ahead. A banner tied to it flapped in the breeze. Damon could see only the colors, but he guessed it marked the hospital tent. They headed for it.

Looking east, they were blinded by the sun as it rose over the top of the makeshift hospital tent. A canopy had been hastily erected, with curtains too light to keep out the weather, should it turn bad.

Damon parted the curtains. Soldiers groaned. Every cot was filled. Many men lay on the floor. "Can we be of service?"

A lone doctor stood over a patient. The apron tied over the doctor's tunic was spattered with blood. "Do you have a wagon?" he asked without more than glancing at them.

"No, I'm afraid not," Damon answered.

"The last of the wagons has left. Some of the more able are carrying the wounded here from the field. What we need is a wagon. They'll bleed to death out there." He tossed his head in the direction of the smoke. "If the enemy doesn't get them first."

Damon threw off his cloak and dipped his hands in the basin. The mud turned the water black. "I can help. I'm a physician. No training in battle wounds, but if you show me what to do . . . "

"There's fresh water just outside."

Damon had forgotten about Artemas until he saw him just inside the entrance. He stood like some giant statue. But he stood. He hadn't fainted. "I can help carry the wounded to you," he said.

"There's no wagon," Damon said.

"I'll carry them, one at a time."

Damon moved close to Artemas and whispered, so the doctor could not hear, "You can't do that."

"Why not?"

"Because if you faint, you'll be vulnerable. The enemy . . . "

"I'll be fine. You help here. I'll help the others."

"It's not dishonorable to be light-headed from the sight of blood. It's common."

"I am not light-headed," Artemas insisted.

"Fine. Thick-headed, then."

Artemas left.

Damon stared at the closed flap for just a moment, then followed outside to scrub off the mud.

"What can I do?" Damon asked when he returned. He held his wet hands away from his mud-caked clothing.

"If you prepare them, I'll stitch them," the doctor said. "Clean the wounds. Remove any arrow tips, broken shafts. Stop the flow of blood with pressure."

Damon began at the nearest cot. He had cut away the man's leather breastplate with a knife and was wrestling with the shaft of an arrow when Artemas came in, followed by two other men, each cradling a wounded soldier. Blood covered Artemas's chest. He gently laid the unconscious man on the floor with the other wounded soldiers.

"Are you all right?" Damon asked him.

"I'm all right. There are at least twenty others out there. Not far. I've got to go." His face was pale, but he stood without wavering and quickly left.

Damon watched the curtain fall back in place behind Artemas. A groan brought him back to the present. He deftly pulled the arrow free and with the heel of his hand applied pressure to the wound.

The doctor and Damon worked steadily. Damon now could tell those wounds that needed attention immediately from those that could wait. He had seen everyone in the tent and knew in what order he should prepare them for the surgeon. He did his best to make them comfortable, moving quickly from patient to patient. The unconscious moaned. There were so many that it sounded like the chants of the priests at the temple of Karnak.

Artemas had brought in seventeen men. Seventeen men he had saved that would have otherwise died. He hadn't fainted. By now he was so covered in blood, Damon wouldn't have recognized him if he had to search him out in the field. Damon looked down and realized he, too, was covered in blood. He'd forgotten his sore muscles.

"Here, tie this tight." The doctor held out the ends of a leather strip wound around a soldier's thigh. Damon tied the leather tight enough to cut into the flesh. The doctor found a saw in the pile of tools beneath the table. "We can't save the leg. We'll have to cut it off. You hold him."

Damon stepped in to hold the man just as Artemas came through the doorway again holding one end of a stretcher. "Look who I found!"

Damon looked at the man lying on the stretcher, then up at Artemas in confusion. Damon had never seen this man before. From his uniform he was obviously an officer. But this couldn't be Caesar. Who else would Artemas be so excited about finding? Then Damon looked into the face of the man carrying the other end of the stretcher. He was smiling. How strange to see a smile amid this blood and gore. It seemed hideously out of place. With his chin Damon motioned where they should put the wounded man, but Artemas didn't move. Annoyed, Damon said, "Can't you see we're about to amputate—" Then he looked at the smiling man again. It couldn't be. But it was. It was his father.

# TWENTY-TWO

His father put down his end of the stretcher and held out his arms. "Son!"

*Son!* That single word hit Damon in the gut as if he had been punched. He felt a fury let loose that made him nearly go blind with its intensity. Son? Who did he think he was, calling Damon *son?* Where was he when Damon had needed him? Where was he when his mother lay dying? When she was in pain? Where was he then? And why had Damon been forced to travel across the sea—barely surviving—to get to this bloody battlefield just so he could tell this—this *father* that his own wife was dead?

"How are things at home? Artemas hasn't told me anything. Leaving it for you, I suspect. How is your mother?"

"Dead."

With satisfaction, Damon watched Litigus's

face. He watched the smile freeze. Then the look of confusion. Then he saw the man, who so wanted to call himself Damon's father, crumple under the weight of that one word.

Litigus looked at his own arms—still out-stretched—as if he wasn't sure what they were and why they were reaching or how to make them do anything else.

"She's dead, Litigus."

Litigus looked again at Damon as if Damon were speaking a language he didn't understand. And then he sat down—*fell* was more like it—on the floor beside the stretcher he had just put down.

Artemas gave Damon a look so full of contempt that Damon stepped back. He'd never seen Artemas look at him that way. Not even when they had been so angry that they hadn't spoken. Damon didn't care. What did Artemas know about a father like Litigus? When Artemas's mother died, his father had been with his family. Artemas didn't understand.

"How . . . did she . . . ?" Litigus looked at Damon with a face like an open wound—raw, disbelieving, full of turmoil.

"There are men who need my care. I'll explain later," Damon said, turning back to assist the physician.

Artemas grabbed his arm and nearly spat his words. "Your father needs you now."

"Well, he'll just have to wait. He can see what *that* feels like."

"I've seen you do a lot of things, Damon. But I've never seen you be cruel. Until now."

"Aren't there more soldiers out in the field who need rescuing?" Damon asked. Then he looked away from Artemas, too.

Damon held the wounded soldier's leg still. The physician seemed unaware of what had passed between Damon and Litigus. His attention was on the thrashing soldier. Damon turned slightly so that he could see Litigus and Artemas without them knowing that he was watching.

Artemas stormed out of the tent. Seconds later Litigus stood, like a man in a dream, and followed—slowly, each movement awkward, as if he had forgotten how to walk.

Through the night Artemas and Damon's father came and went. They worked in silence. Each time his father entered the hospital tent, Damon could feel his presence, even before he saw him. Each time his father looked more stooped. Once, when Damon thought Litigus might be going to speak to him, Damon turned quickly, busying himself dressing a wound that he would later only have to re-dress. He had nothing more to say to Litigus.

It was near dawn, and Damon didn't think his legs would hold him up much longer. The physician's eyes were rimmed in red. They would have to take turns sleeping soon. They couldn't keep this up. They needed to get these men to a real hospital. They were running out of supplies as quickly as they were running out of the strength to treat the flow of wounded.

Just as Damon was about to suggest to the physician that he rest for a few hours, the tent flap parted and Artemas came in carrying yet another soldier. Damon put his face in his hands and asked Thoth for strength. He was so weary he wasn't sure he could shift the men to make room for another soldier. But Artemas did not lay this man down with the others. He brought him directly to Damon. Damon felt the flutter of panic in his chest when he saw the pain in Artemas's eyes. He was afraid to look. Afraid not to.

"He called for you before he collapsed."

What had Damon done? This was all his fault.

# TWENTY-THREE

Lay him here. Gently." Damon cleared a table, sweeping jars and bandages to the floor.

Artemas cradled Damon's father's head in the crook of his arm while he lowered him to the table. Damon folded his cloak for a headrest and then pressed his ear to his father's chest.

"Is he—?"

Damon silenced Artemas with a raised hand.

At first Damon heard nothing. But then one beat. Then another. Uneven. Faltering. But beating. "He's alive." *But for how long?*

He lifted his father's arm, searching the shoulder for wounds. *His skin feels so cold and clammy. He looks gray, not like the others, who paled from the blood loss. He looks gray.*

Artemas straightened the scabbard at Damon's father's belt. "He was carrying another soldier, protecting him with his own body. From the armor the man was wearing, I'd say he was a legate."

"Legate?"

"His commanding officer. He's dead. I'm going back for him."

"Don't." Damon grabbed Artemas by the arm. "Don't risk your life for a dead man."

"We can't leave him for the enemy. Your father understood that."

"And look where that got him." Damon grabbed a blanket from under a cot and spread it over his father. He called to the physician, "I need help over here!" When he looked back, Artemas was gone.

"There's nothing we can do for him. It's his heart," the physician said, with nothing more than a glance.

"There must be something!" Damon shouted at the physician's back. His heart! Damon had broken it—he knew it. He had wanted to hurt his father. Hurt him like Damon had been hurt. But not this. Damon hadn't meant for this to happen. "You can't just let him die!"

The physician turned with a questioning look.

"He's . . ." Damon looked at Litigus, then without looking back at the physician said, "He's my father."

"I'm sorry. It's between him and his gods now. I can stitch a wound. I can sometimes remove an offending limb and save the man. But there is no way to mend a failing heart."

"No spell?"

The physician shook his head. "I'm sorry." He returned to his operating table.

Damon wrung out a cloth dipped in water and swabbed his father's neck and arms. "I'm here, Father. I'm here." His father lay so still that Damon kept putting his ear to his chest to be sure the heart still beat, each time holding his breath for fear he would hear nothing. "I'm here."

Damon groped for the amulet around his neck, then remembered it was with his mother. He searched through the pouch tied to his belt and pulled out the stone Cleopatra had given him. With his thumb he rubbed the carved surface of the wadjet eye and recited the healing chants. He begged Horus to make his father's heart speak out again.

Damon closed his eyes. He was startled to see behind his closed eyelids the god Bes waving a sword and sticking his tongue out of his lion's mouth.

Damon opened his eyes and listened again to his father's heart. It fluttered. Then beat. Then was quiet. Damon pressed his ear harder. There it was, faintly.

Damon closed his eyes and Bes appeared again. Damon wanted to shout at the image. *Go away. Take your sword.* Then he remembered a story about Bes his mother had told him when he was little. God of family. Strange little god. But his sword repelled danger. Damon squeezed his eyes shut and watched the dwarf–god Bes dance behind his eyelids, all the while stroking the stone.

When Artemas entered the tent carrying the dead legate, Damon silently thanked Isis that Artemas was safe. Artemas slumped in the corner still holding the man in his arms. There was nowhere to put him down.

Damon stood quietly and shifted two stretchers to make room for the man. He strung a torn cloak between tent posts so the men could not see what had befallen their leader. He looked back at his father. He looked so old. And fragile. How could he have said those things to him? This wasn't the giant he remembered. This man was no bigger than Artemas. Did six years make such a difference? He took his father's hand in his own, pressing the amulet between their palms.

Artemas sat in the corner, his head drooping, his arms resting on his knees. The physician rubbed a damp cloth across the back of his own neck and stretched his shoulder by rotating his arm. How long had the man been without sleep? Days, Damon was sure. Sleep. They all needed sleep.

The groans of the soldiers had quieted. Or had

Damon grown used to them? He felt his head bob. He jerked it up. He couldn't sleep. Not yet. He prayed to Ra to give him the chance to tell his father he was sorry. He prayed their last words spoken on earth weren't those he had shouted in anger. *Just one more chance, Ra. One more.*

Damon snapped his head back. He'd fallen asleep. His father groaned and rolled his head from side to side. Damon stroked his brow. "I'm here, Father." He gripped his father's hand in his own. Pressed between their palms, the wadjet eye felt warm, with the Pharaoh's own heat.

His father blinked. "My Seshet?"

Damon blinked back tears—the first tears he had shed. His father was calling for his wife. Did he see Mother in the otherworld? Did his father have one foot in each world?

"No, it's not Seshet," Damon whispered.

"You have her eyes—" His own eyes rolled back in his head. Damon fell to his father's breast and listened frantically. It was there. The heart spoke. Was he imagining? Was the heartbeat a bit stronger? A bit more regular?

He put a hand to his father's cheek. It felt warmer. He sensed the physician standing behind him.

"It's still too soon to tell, but this return of natural skin color is a good omen," the doctor said. "The evil spirits have deserted his flesh."

Damon dared not hope. He feared it would be bad luck to hope.

His father opened his eyes again. Damon watched him struggle to keep the lids open. His eyes rolled back in the sockets, his eyelids fluttered. Then he lifted his brow, opening one eye with effort. He looked at Damon.

"Damon?"

"Yes, Father. I'm here."

His father smiled before he slipped from consciousness again. Damon felt his father grip his hand. Could he forgive Damon? Could Damon forgive himself?

# TWENTY-FOUR

It had been two days since the wagons had come to move the wounded to field hospitals. Sleep had finally come for Damon—at first in snatches, but then he had given in to it and slept soundly at his father's bedside.

Artemas had gone to deliver Cleopatra's scroll to Caesar at the first sunrise. Word was that the mighty Caesar was just outside camp and on his way, but Artemas had not been able to wait.

Damon was getting restless, waiting for the physician to come check on his father again. His father was still unconscious, and Damon worried what that might mean. He had known patients who never returned from the twilight.

Artemas rushed down the row of cots toward him. "He said, 'Thank you, Artemas.' Caesar said my name. 'Artemas.'" Artemas rolled the syllables as if testing his name for the first time, as if he had never heard it spoken before Caesar said it. "He knew my name. Imagine it!"

"That's a wonder. Now hush, you'll disturb him." Damon gestured toward his father.

"Yes, yes. You are right. I should be quiet." Artemas squatted near the foot of the cot, then bounced up again. "He touched me right here." Artemas showed Damon his shoulder as if it were something to look at.

Damon nodded. "Yes. It looks different now. Golden almost. Would you be quiet?"

"You're making fun of me." Artemas peered at his shoulder, flexing it, admiring it from different angles. "It *does* look different." He grinned.

"Artemas, this is a hospital. People here are not well. You are acting like a baboon."

"You're just jealous."

"I'm sure that's it." Damon shook his head. Sometimes Artemas behaved like a child.

A soldier on a nearby cot raised himself to one elbow and whispered to Artemas, "He touched me once, too." The soldier rubbed his forearm as if he could still feel the touch.

"Did he know your name?"

The soldier smiled. "Caesar knows everyone's name."

The soldier looked wistfully at his arm, and

Artemas looked at his shoulder. Damon rolled his eyes.

"It really *is* you," Damon's father said weakly. "I wasn't dreaming."

Damon leaned over the cot. "It really is."

"I was afraid to believe you would stay."

"I was afraid you would never know that I stayed."

His father smiled and clutched Damon's hand. His squeeze was weak, but just because it lacked strength didn't mean it lacked power. Damon felt his arm tingle right up to his scalp.

Damon smoothed his father's brow. "I was scared that I would never be able to tell you that I loved you."

His father tried to lift himself up, but his face drained of color and he winced.

Damon quickly eased him back flat. "I'm so sorry. This is all my fault, if I hadn't—"

"What's all your fault?" his father asked.

"Your heart . . . I . . . what I said . . ."

"This is not the first time my heart has given me trouble. Sometimes my chest feels as if one of your Egyptian hippos is sitting on it, and my arm pains me so I can't pull my sword from its sheath." Litigus coughed. When the spasm passed he said, "You are not to blame."

"I thought I had broken it." Damon lowered his eyes in shame.

"Your being here mends it." His father squeezed Damon's fingers again, and the two held on to each other.

Artemas stepped back into the shadows, smiling.

# TWENTY-FIVE

Trumpets blared.

"What's that?" Damon asked.

"It must be Caesar," his father said. "He never forgets his men." His father had been looking stronger these past few days, but at the mention of Caesar the color flushed his cheeks ruddy and he looked almost robust. Together they stared at the doorway.

Caesar entered the hospital, pausing at each bed. He was taller than Damon had expected. He wore a laurel wreath on his head. Damon had heard it was to hide his baldness. When Caesar neared Damon's father, he smiled warmly, but there was an authority in his dark eyes that held Damon rigid.

"Litigus, my friend, you have a fine son here. My surgeon informs me that these young men saved many of my soldiers."

A cheer rose from the men in the tent. Damon felt himself blush.

Caesar turned to Damon. "Your father has served me well these twenty-five years. We have fought many a battle side by side. Had I a legion of men like Litigus, the world could be Rome's."

"The world *will* be Rome's, with Caesar as general." Litigus saluted Caesar, thumping his chest with a closed fist.

Caesar extended one hand toward Damon. "I don't suppose you would consider filling the void my army will suffer when your father retires?"

Damon smiled and shook his head. "I'm no soldier. I wish only to return to my studies."

"Perhaps you?" Caesar asked Artemas.

"But I'm Greek."

"Then the auxiliary troops. We need navy men. You will be a Roman citizen when you are done. Interested?"

Damon was afraid that Artemas would jump over the cot to join up this very instant. When Artemas was quiet, Damon looked back to see why. He was frozen, speechless. Damon stepped back and elbowed Artemas. "Say something," he said out of the side of his mouth.

"It would be an honor," Artemas blurted.

"Litigus, don't scare him off with tales of how you centurion instructors torture these fellows for four months and call it training." Caesar patted his centurion's ankle. "I expect you to invite me to dinner in your villa back home in Italy when you have put your pension to good use."

"You'll eat me out of half my pension, no doubt." Litigus tried to laugh at his own joke but ended up coughing.

"I'll do my best. How else can I recover my expenses?" Caesar winked at Damon. "Be well, Litigus." Damon sensed that Caesar was leaving because he knew Litigus would not rest as long as his commander stayed. He was surprised by Caesar's sensitivity. It seemed that soldiers were nothing like what he had thought.

They watched Caesar go. When the tent flap had fallen into place behind the last tribune, Damon turned to Artemas. "Congratulations. I guess you'll be more than a paper soldier, after all. Don't you wish we could rub that in the gubernator's face?"

Artemas laughed. "I do."

"We won't be returning to Egypt together."

The smile faded from Artemas's face. "No, I guess we won't."

"The journey home won't be the same," Damon said.

"Perhaps that's a good thing."

Damon laughed. "It is indeed a good thing. I've had enough adventure."

They stood facing each other, unsure of what to say next.

"You'll need gear. A soldier supplies his own gear," Litigus said, looking from Damon to Artemas and smiling softly.

Artemas smacked his forehead with his palm. "You are right, but I haven't any money. My gold's at the bottom of the sea."

Litigus cleared his throat. "You are a bit bigger than I am, but the ties can be loosened, and a gladius knows no size. You shall have my gear."

"I couldn't take your armor."

"Why not? I doubt a cotton farmer needs a breastplate and helmet, nor a sword."

"They grow cotton in Italy?" Damon asked.

"They do in Egypt."

"But your pension! You've worked twenty-five years for that farm."

"I've worked twenty-five years so that I can have time with my family. You are my family."

Damon didn't trust his voice. He gripped his father's hand in his own.

"Good. Then it's settled." Litigus reached under his cot with his free hand and retrieved his gladius in its scabbard. He held it out to Artemas. "It was with this sword I earned the title 'centurion.'"

"I don't know how I can ever repay you."

"Be a good soldier."

"Yes, sir."

Artemas threw an arm around Damon's shoulder and squeezed hard. "We will see each other again in Egypt."

*Egypt*, Damon thought. She seemed a world away. It would be good to get home.

# GLOSSARY

**Alexander the Great** — 356–323 B.C., king of Macedonia and conqueror of much of the civilized world, including Egypt.

**amphora** — a large two-handled jar for storing wine or grains.

**amulet** — a small charm worn for protection or luck.

**Anubis** — the jackal-headed god of embalming. The Egyptians believed that when someone died, Anubis weighed the person's heart against the feather of truth. If the deceased had been good during his earthly life, his heart would be light and would balance favorably with the feather of truth. Osiris, the king of the dead, would then admit the deceased into the otherworld.

**Apollo** — Greek and Roman god of healing, music, and poetry.

**ba** — the soul.

**Beautiful House** — place where embalmers mummified the dead.

**Book of the Dead** — funerary texts; spells to help the dead pass safely through the underworld on their journey to the afterlife.

**brazier** — heater.

**Byblos** — a territory of Egypt.

**Caesar** — 100–44 B.C., one of the greatest generals in history; Roman statesman and historian.

**centurion** — a legionnaire promoted to command because of bravery. Centurions trained troops and maintained discipline.

**Charmion** — Cleopatra's head lady-in-waiting, chosen as a companion from the nobility. They became close friends.

**Cicero** — 106–43 B.C., a lawyer and statesman known as Rome's greatest orator.

**Circus Maximus** — the largest entertainment building in Rome. Gladiator competitions and chariot races were held there.

**Cleopatra** — 69–30 B.C., last Pharaoh of Egypt.

**cross to the other bank** — a common euphemism for death.

**Eye of Horus** — Egyptian symbol believed to ensure good health.

**fenugreek** — a plant used for healing.

**Field of Reeds** — Egyptian heaven.

**Forum** — the central meeting place and focus of public life in Rome.

**galley** — a warship propelled by oars.

**gladiators** — slaves, men condemned to death, prisoners of war, and professionals trained for combat in duels to the death for the entertainment of the bloodthirsty Roman public.

**gladius** — a sword used in hand–to–hand combat.

**gubernator** — Latin for "sailing master"; the steersman of the ship.

**Herodotus** — a Greek historian in the 5th century B.C.

**hieroglyphs** — "sacred inscriptions," a writing system in which symbols represent sounds, similar to an alphabet.

**Hippocrates** — 460?–380? B.C., a Greek physician.

**Isis** — Egyptian goddess of protection.

**iugula** — Latin for "Slit his throat," shouted by the crowds at a gladiator duel, meaning that the combatant should die.

**Jove** — also known as Jupiter, father of the gods to the Romans.

**ka** — spiritual essence. Egyptians believed the ka to be a spiritual twin that existed alongside, yet separate from, its human host. At the time of death the ka entered the underworld before the body, in order to prepare for their rejoining. Egyptians referred to death as "going to one's ka."

**Karnak** — site in Egypt of the largest temple in the world.

**legate** — commander of a legion, often from the senatorial class.

**legion** — a division of the Roman army, consisting of five thousand to six thousand soldiers.

**legionnaire** — a career Roman soldier. Upon retiring after twenty-five years of service, a legionnaire received a pension, often in the form of land.

**Mercury heap** — along Roman roads statues of Mercury, ancient Roman god who was the patron of travelers, were often surrounded by piles of stones tossed by travelers offering homage.

**mile** — short of today's mile, a thousand military paces (approximately five thousand feet).

**milestone** — one of the thousand-pound stone pillars placed alongside Roman roads carved with the name of the road, the emperor who built or maintained the road, and the distances to key stops along the road.

**mitte** — Latin for "Send him back," shouted by the crowd at a gladiator duel, meaning that the combatant's life should be spared.

**Munda** — site of Caesar's battle in Spain in 45 B.C.

**murmillon** — type of heavily armed gladiator, symbolic of the fish.

**Museum** — academy in Egypt devoted to the Muses, where academics pursued the sciences and the arts. Scholars in anatomy, astronomy, geography, geometry, medicine, philosophy, and rhetoric were supported by the Pharaoh.

**myrrh** — an incense used in the ritual of mummification.

**natron** — salts used to dry the bodies in the mummification process.

**Nubia** — a region at Egypt's southern border.

**Olympus** — Cleopatra's personal physician and lecturer at the Museum in Alexandria.

**Osiris** — Egyptian god of the underworld, who judged all people when they died.

**Ostia** — from the word meaning "entrance," Roman port and trading center located at the mouth of the Tiber.

**palm wine** — a fluid used to cleanse the body during mummification.

**Pharaoh** — the king of Egypt, thought to be a god.

**Poseidon** — Greek god of the sea.

**Praxagoras** — Greek physician who, around 340 B.C., discovered the role of arteries and veins in circulation of the blood.

**Ptolemy** — the name of all the Pharaohs belonging to the Greek dynasty that ruled Egypt from 323 to 30 B.C. Cleopatra's brother and husband.

**Ra** — Egyptian sun god. Also spelled Re.

**Red Land** — the Egyptian desert.

**retiarius** — type of lightly armed gladiator, symbolic of the fisherman.

**scarab** — a beetle.

**scribe** — a person whose job was to write. Since the Egyptian language had more than 700 hieroglyphs, training lasted five to ten years, beginning when the scribe was as young as nine years old.

**shabti** — "the answerers," funerary figurines placed in Egyptian tombs to serve the gods for the deceased.

**Thoth** — Egyptian ibis-headed god of wisdom.

**Tiber** — river running through Rome to the Mediterranean at Ostia.

**Tiro** — Cicero's freedman.

**Via Sacra** — "Sacred Way," central Roman road.

**vortex** — a whirlpool. Many fables describe the vortex off the coast of Sicily.

**wadjet eye** — "healthy eye"; see Eye of Horus.

**Zela** — battle that inspired Caesar's famous words *"Veni, vidi, vici"*—"I came, I saw, I conquered."

# AUTHOR'S NOTE

The ancient Mediterranean was a culturally complex world. The three dominant cultures—Greek, Roman, and Egyptian—were often at odds because of their deeply rooted differences. The Romans saw themselves as moral and frugal and thought the Egyptians excessive and lewd, but they tolerated them because they needed Egypt's grain. The Egyptians and the Greeks considered the Romans drab and barbaric, but they tolerated them because of the Roman Empire's military strength. Only the Egyptians and the Greeks seemed able to mix comfortably. Even their religions meshed: Egyptian gods had Greek counterparts.

## ALEXANDRIA

The city of Alexandria, in Egypt, was built by a culture that revered physical beauty and grandeur. It was a feast for the eyes, boasting public parks and gardens, grand boulevards a hundred feet wide, and towering buildings and monuments of white stone. The Library and the Museum, located in the Royal Quarter, distinguished Alexandria as a center of learning. The Museum was dedicated to the nine Muses, Greek goddesses of arts and sciences. Supported by the Royal House, scholars gathered there to pursue their studies, free from financial worries. Olympus, Cleopatra's personal physician, studied and taught at the Museum. It was there that Herophilus discovered that the brain—not the heart, as previously believed—was the center of intelligence. Rumors that he cut open living subjects to study internal organs have been neither substantiated nor disproved.

In 45 B.C. Alexandria was a cosmopolitan center of commerce, the hub of caravan routes, and a thriving port. Over half a million people of many races and religions lived there. The markets overflowed with goods from all over the world—silks from the Orient, wines from Greece, glass from Venice. With its international flavor, Alexandria had little in common with the rest of Egypt.

Homes in Alexandria were separated by courtyard walls. Within these walls, gardens were often planted around a well dug in the center. Wood, which was not grown in Alexandria, and could not be grown in the nearby desert, was scarce and only the very wealthy could afford to import it, so homes were built from clay and stone, and gates were made of iron.

The exact layout of Alexandria is unknown but has been pieced together from accounts such as that found in Strabo's *Geography*. Strabo, who lived at the time of this book's setting, was a Greek who traveled extensively, describing the places he visited in a seventeen-volume work entitled *Geography*. It is believed he arrived in Alexandria around 27 B.C. In contrast, detailed maps of ancient Rome still survive. Compared with the splendor of Alexandria, Rome surely must have appeared like a slum to travelers such as Damon and Artemas. Its crowded streets and drab earth colors would have seemed mundane indeed compared with the brilliant white of Alexandria.

## DEATH

For thousands of years, the Egyptians buried their dead in the desert. The dry sands perfectly mummified the bodies—assuming jackals and hyenas didn't get them first. The Egyptians believed that the body must remain intact after death, or else the ka would be condemned to roam the desert for eternity.

Embalming the body preserved it for the ka in the otherworld. Burial preparations were customarily made in the Beautiful House, the equivalent of our present-day funeral home. The procedure could be as simple as stuffing the corpse with sawdust and wrapping it in linen, or as elaborate as crafting a gem-encrusted, solid-gold sarcophagus in the likeness of the deceased.

The most detailed primary source describing the process was written by Herodotus, a Greek historian, four hundred years before this story takes place. Embalmers first removed all the internal organs except the heart. The brain, considered worthless, was picked out through the nostrils and discarded; the other organs were wrapped in packages to be stored in Canopic jars. The body cavity was then cleansed and packed with natron to dry. When dry, the shriveled carcass was stuffed with sawdust and herbs and wrapped in linen soaked in glue. Amulets were often wrapped with the mummy to protect it on its journey.

Despite the Egyptians' belief that the otherworld was a place of enchantment, they didn't like to use the word *death*. The Valley of the Kings, where the Pharaohs were buried, was located on the other side of the Nile from where the Egyptians lived. When they wanted to communicate that someone had died, they would say that the deceased had "crossed to the other bank."

Although the title sounds gloomy, the Book of the Dead was actually an instruction book for the joyful survival of the soul. In it there were chants and spells to guide the dead through the underworld and equip them with all that was needed to obtain eternal happiness in the Field of Reeds, the Egyptian heaven. The family of the deceased would commission a scribe to write on scrolls of papyrus specific spells chosen from the nearly two hundred available. The scroll would then be wrapped in the bandages of the mummy along with amulets for guidance and protection.

There were spells for every imaginable purpose. One spell was designed to empower the figurines known as *shabti*. The Egyptians viewed the otherworld as agricultural, like their own, with fields needing to be plowed, sowed, and harvested. The shabti acted as substitute workers, relieving the dead of hard labor.

## MEDICINE

Medicine in ancient times was a combination of science and superstition. The Egyptians were advanced in their understanding of how the body worked and in their use of medicinal herbs, and yet they still clung to many old beliefs. A physician might adroitly set a broken bone—and then chant to the gods of healing to mend the break. Some of the medicines of old are being reconsidered and are finding a place in modern medical practice. Maggots are still used today to remove dead tissue. They are efficient at their task and would probably be more widely used if people didn't find them repugnant.

Medicine often advances in the fields where physicians have opportunity to practice. Egypt, having been in relative peace in the years following Alexander's conquest, did not have physicians as experienced in caring for battle wounds as Rome did. It was not uncommon for Egyptian physicians to travel to Rome to learn methods for treating injuries suffered in war.

## TRAVEL

Traveling in the ancient world was challenging. There were no commercial passenger ships as there are today. Travelers hitched a ride aboard whatever vessel was heading where they wanted to go. They brought everything they needed for the voyage, including bedding, cooking pots, and food. Although storms were always a concern, pirates had been cleared away by Pompey years before, so travel had become much safer.

The Greeks were known for wonderful seaworthy

vessels, whereas the Romans were more comfortable on land than on water. The ships one might see in Alexandria's harbor ranged in size from the enormous cargo vessel used for transporting grain to Rome, to papyrus boats, so small they were more like floats that an Egyptian boy might use for pleasure or fishing. Ships were equipped with large square sails made of linen. The type of galley that Damon and Artemas traveled on had three levels: the upper deck, where passengers were expected to sleep and cook (in the open); the first level, where the gubernator and the captain had cabins; and the belly, where the oarsmen lived, shoulder to shoulder. The conditions below were so foul that disease was common, and rare was the voyage that didn't cost many oarsmen their lives.

Ships did not travel in the winter, not because of inclement weather, but because winter skies were often overcast, making navigation by the stars difficult.

Sailors were superstitious. Everything was seen as an omen. Sometimes ships did not leave port on the designated day because of a "sign." To sneeze on the gangplank meant dangerous seas, owls meant pirate attacks, and goats meant a storm—the darker the goat, the bigger the storm.

Travel by road in the Roman Empire was common and relatively comfortable. Rome's roads were among the finest feats of engineering in the ancient world. They were built by and for the Roman army and were designed to withstand all weather conditions. First the ground was carefully prepared for stability and to prevent erosion. Then huge polygonal paving stones were fit tightly together like a jigsaw puzzle, with the center of the road raised slightly so that rainwater would flow off to the sides. Then any cracks were packed with sand. Although the Romans tried to make the most of the natural terrain, if necessary they would cut into hillsides or dig tunnels rather than deviate too far from the most direct route.

Every Roman mile (one thousand five-foot paces), a marker indicating distances to different towns was placed along the road. The golden milestone, located in the Forum in Rome, was so named because the mileage to key cities was gilded on the stone.

In addition to the milestones along the road, there were also small shrines to Mercury, the patron of traveler. Passersby would toss a stone onto the pile to pay homage to the god. These mounds of stones came to be known as Mercury heaps.

### CLEOPATRA, CAESAR, AND CICERO

The portrayal of Cleopatra in this story is based on the descriptions left by her own physician and the historian Plutarch. According to these accounts, she was not particularly beautiful. She was intelligent and ambitious and had a wonderful sense of humor. Her voice must have been melodic, for those who heard it never failed to mention its hypnotic tenor. Cleopatra had an affinity for languages and spoke at least a dozen; she was the only Pharaoh in the Ptolemy line the (Greek line of Pharaohs that followed Alexander's conquest in 332 B.C.) to learn Egyptian. She was known to be deeply inquisitive;

149

nothing was too inconsequential to capture her full attention. Although Cleopatra did not have a drop of Egyptian blood in her, she adopted the Egyptian goddess Isis as her patron. This embracing of the Egyptian way of life, in the end, endeared her to her people.

The Romans viewed the Egyptians as ostentatious. To them Cleopatra represented the excessiveness of her country. They accused her of seducing Caesar and polluting his thoughts. It is hard to believe there is any truth to the idea that Cleopatra could corrupt the philandering Caesar, who was years her senior and hardly an innocent. Much of the surviving information about Cleopatra was written by her enemies, the Romans, coloring our impressions of her.

In the early months of 45 B.C., Caesar fought the battle of Munda, the end of a brutal campaign in Spain. At that time, Caesar was the most powerful man in the known world. His formidable leadership abilities had earned him a brilliant political and military career. He was said to be the greatest general since Alexander. He earned the loyalty of the men he vanquished as well as those he commanded. In the battlefield, Caesar lived like his men, without special privileges. He knew their names, their families, their histories, and in return he was loved by them. One of Caesar's most admirable traits was his ability to forgive his enemies and be gracious in victory. His one insecurity was about his receding hairline, which he masked by wearing a laurel wreath.

Cicero was without doubt the finest orator of

Roman times. His talent led him to law, and he was at his best when arguing cases before a jury. He was quoted as saying that a trial lawyer's skill lies in his ability to "throw dust in a juryman's eyes."

In Rome, greedy landlords were building the tinderbox that would burn under Nero. Using inferior materials and unsafe designs, builders threw tenements together to house the growing population. Cicero's conviction that it was the duty of the upper class to protect the rights of all makes it plausible that he might have argued a case against the landlords.

Cicero's disapproval of Cleopatra was public knowledge. Since Cleopatra held men of learning in high esteem, she must have been particularly hurt by this cultured man's snubbing.

Although Cicero's political support of Caesar was fickle at best, Caesar was generous to enemies he respected. He expressed his admiration for Cicero's work by saying that Cicero's pushing back the frontiers of the mind was more important to the Republic than his own conquests of land.

## WARFARE

The Roman army was highly organized and efficient. It was made up of units called legions, each consisting of five thousand to six thousand men. The legions were subdivided into centuries, each consisting of about eighty men. Each century was commanded by a centurion, who was commanded by a tribune, who was commanded by a legate. Leadership posts were filled by the wealthier class.

Centurion instructors subjected new recruits to a grueling four-month basic training, where soldiers learned to run carrying sixty pounds of gear for as far as thirty miles. Mobility was essential to an army's ability to surprise the enemy and engage them unprepared.

Roman soldiers provided their own weapons and armor, making equipment far from standard. The wealthier the soldier, the better his gear. Although enlistment at this time was no longer dependent on financial status, Roman citizenship was required. Career military men were given generous pensions, often in the form of farms.

Egypt's army was not as discriminating as Rome's. It recruited debtors and criminals in an attempt to bolster numbers. Cleopatra was also trying to build a navy, but the endeavor took years. Lumber was scarce, and all the large timbers used to build ships had to be brought via the Mediterranean from Byblos (near Beirut).

### THE CIRCUS MAXIMUS

At the Circus Maximus in Rome, games always ended in death—death for the animals, death for the gladiators, death for the entertainers. That such depravity was considered entertaining must have sickened outsiders like Damon and Artemas. Many historians now attribute the Romans' lust for these excessively violent spectacles to insanity caused by lead poisoning. The Romans drank from goblets made of a metal alloy that contained lead.

The games at the Circus Maximus usually were held

in the daytime before crowds numbering as many as a quarter million. The most popular event was the chariot race, but as the population developed an increasing delight in gladiator combat, the Romans eventually built the Coliseum. The opening performances there continued nonstop for one hundred days, costing hundreds of gladiators and thousands of animals their lives.

While the Greek games honored the body and the Egyptians abhorred killing for sport, the Romans sought entertainment in bloodlust, accentuating basic cultural differences, deepening mutual distrust, and straining already brittle relationships. Nowhere was the clash of cultures more evident than in the inhuman brutality at the Circus Maximus.

# BIBLIOGRAPHY

The very first bibliographies were created to catalog the Library of Alexandria's 700,000 scrolls.

Allen, Thomas B. *Shadows in the Sea*. New York: Lyons & Buford, 1996.

Casson, Lionel. *Travel in the Ancient World*. Baltimore: Johns Hopkins University Press, 1994.

Connolly, Peter, and Hazel Dodge. *The Ancient City: Life in Classical Athens and Rome*. Oxford: Oxford University Press, 1998.

Davison, Michael. *The Glory of Greece and the World of Alexander*. New York: Abbeville Press, 1980.

Faulkner, Raymond O. *The Ancient Egyptian Book of the Dead*. Austin: University of Texas Press, 1997.

Foreman, Laura. *Cleopatra's Palace: In Search of a Legend*. New York: Random House, 1999.

Foster, E. M. *Alexandria: A History and a Guide*. Garden City, N.Y.: Anchor Books, 1961.

Freeman, Charles. *Egypt, Greece, and Rome: Civilizations of the Ancient Mediterranean*. New York: Oxford University Press, 1996.

Goodenough, Simon. *Egyptian Mythology*. New York: Michael J. Friedman/Fairfax Publishers, 1997.

Grant, Michael. *The World of Rome*. New York: Penguin Books, 1960.

Hamilton, Edith. *The Greek Way.* New York: W. W. Norton, 1930.

Herodotus. *The Histories.* Translated by Robin Waterfield. Oxford: Oxford University Press, 1998.

Heuer, Kenneth. *City of the Stargazers.* New York: Charles Scribner's Sons, 1972.

*Hippocratic Writings.* Translated by Francis Adams. Chicago: William Benton, 1952.

Liberati, Anna Maria, and Fabio Bourbon. *Ancient Rome: History of a Civilization That Ruled the World.* New York: Stewart, Tabori & Chang, 1996.

Montet, Pierre. *Everyday Life in Egypt.* Philadelphia: University of Pennsylvania Press, 1981.

Plutarch. *Lives.* Translated by Bernadotte Perrin. Loeb Classical Library. Cambridge: Harvard University Press, 1914.

Sandison, David. *The Art of Ancient Egypt.* San Diego: Laurel Glen, 1997.

*Strabo's Geography: Book 17.* Translated by Horace Leonard Jones and edited by G. P. Goold. Loeb Classical Library. Cambridge: Harvard University Press, 1996.

Weigall, Arthur. *The Life and Times of Cleopatra, Queen of Egypt: A Study in the Origin of the Roman Empire.* New York: G. P. Putnam's Sons, 1924.

Wilson, Keith D. *Cause of Death: A Writer's Guide to Death, Murder and Forensic Medicine.* Cincinnati: Writer's Digest Books, 1992.

Zambucka, Kristin. *Cleopatra: Goddess/Queen.* Honolulu: Harrane, 1989.